THE TIME AFTER OBLIVION

MYTHOS BOOK 1

JONNY CAPPS

INTRODUCTION

When I sleep, I dream. Within those dreams, I am escorted into another realm. I transcend reality and enter a world that is unknown to mankind, existing behind the barrier. When I was young, it used to terrify me. I was unclear as to which was true reality, and which was my dream. In my teen years, I discovered the truth: my dreams were not truly dreams, but rather visions of a dimension that humanity was not prepared for, nor could they understand. I was seeing visions of another world, existing alongside our own.

One night, while channeling in this distant, neighboring realm, the great sun god, Ra, came to me. He told me that there were things that he needed me to see. Taking hold of my shoulder, he flew with me over plains and waters, revealing to me things that I could have never imagined. He showed me that the gods of myth were not only real, but existing with us, gently guiding and controlling cultures. As he revealed these things to me, I was astonished by what I saw. The great gods of old, ruthless and savage, governed humanity. Their influence was in everything, from Parliament to Saturday morning cartoons. They stayed behind their curtain, awaiting the time when they could reveal themselves and bring about the destruction of the human age, guiding us into a new age of mythology. Ra revealed to me that it was my destiny to prepare humanity for this time. I was chosen as the scribe of the gods, and it was up to me to document their tales.

As we flew over the Lilliputian colonies (Jonathan Swift was a god-scribe, too) in the waters of the Atlantic, Ra sensed a great force beneath us. He tried to protect us by detouring, but it was too late. The goddess Hecate attacked us with her dark magic, striking Ra. Ra fought back with his sun-god powers, but he had been struck too harshly. He fell toward the waters. As we fell, Hecate took hold of me. She warned me that it would be detrimental to reveal these things to humanity. They were not ready to see the truth. I would be no scribe, but rather a harbinger of doom. Humanity could not know the secret workings of the gods. I had not been given a gift, but rather a curse, to see these things. She released me then, to plummet to my death in the bowels of the Krakan who had suddenly appeared beneath us, its savage jaws awaiting our imminent doom.

I awoke screaming. Scarlet Johansson told me to shut up and go back to sleep.

Obviously, that's complete horse crap. "Mythos" was originally inspired by a thirty-second scene in a bad '90s movie.

Just to be clear, I don't actually believe in or worship these gods. If someone else wants to start a religion based on my books, I would be okay with that. Please don't expect me to be at your meetings.

—*Jonny Capps*

Dedicated to the cat burglar who sits outside my window.

PROLOGUE

Passage through the Mists of Time is not as difficult as one would think. Really, if one simply focuses on their destination, it is easy to navigate. That is, of course, as long as the destination contains no distractions. Inevitably, distractions will crop up. Then, the journey becomes more complex, dangerous, even. Still, that is not Time's fault. The travelers are the ones who decide to stray from the straightforward road in search of adventure, thrills, or opportunity. Most are still able to navigate their path to some certainty, and most reach their destination, more or less, in one piece. It is, after all, human nature to survive.

In a frozen corner of Time, three sisters sit. They have sat there since the Beginning, and they will continue to sit there until they are done with their task. The first is a beautiful young blond with eyes as blue as the sky and lips as full and red as fresh strawberries, but surely tasting twice as sweet. She begins the task by pulling the Thread. Supporting it, she passes the Thread to her sister. This woman is middle-aged and plump, but with eyes that shine with matronly love. She accepts the Thread and studies it. She continues to pull it away from the first sister until she has found an exact spot on the string. She then points to the area and passes the Thread to the third sister. This woman, old, wrinkled, and crone-like, takes no pleasure in her task. Her vacant eyes hold no emotion at all as she brings the macabre razor in her hand to the area and severs the Thread.

Once the Thread has been cut, the process begins again.

CHAPTER ONE

I

THICK CLOUD COVER, HERALDING AN APPROACHING STORM, obscured the sun. The ear-piercing screech of a carrion bird tore through the air. Any who heard it would know that it signaled a recent or approaching death, as if the bird were saying a blessing over its meal before it dined. Neither man nor beast mattered to the fowl; it only knew that the natural order was soon to provide a meal.

The residents of the coastal city, Aigio, knew the sound well. Aigio was a coastal town on the Gulf of Corinth. It relied on exporting fish as well as fruits grown in the hills clustered around the city. Like many cities, Aigio had its athletes, its smiths and carpenters, but its main claim to notoriety was the luscious fruit. Without the export of fruit, the town's economy would collapse. This made the arrival of a particularly bloodthirsty beast even more troubling. The beast, a chimera, had situated itself between the town and its crop. A few men from the town risked the beast for the sake of the harvest. Their blood stained the ground. Aigio's desperate mayor chose to outsource the task of dealing with the beast, rather than risk losing more of his residents. Were the heroes successful in their venture, a few coins would be an acceptable sacrifice to be rid of the nuisance. If (or, more likely, when) the beast killed them, the town would preserve its numbers. Perhaps the beast would even consume enough to be satisfied for a time, allowing the town to harvest its fruit for a brief time.

Although, should they witness the chimera devouring the champions, the mayor doubted Aigio held men brave enough to attempt it.

The beast was huge. With the body of a gigantic lion, it stood nearly ten feet from the ground. Its tail was a python that wrapped and swirled its way around any nearby attackers. Should there be none close, it would spew fire from its mouth to incinerate assailants at range. Atop the lion's head, emerging from beneath the mane and behind the ears, ram's horns sprouted, threatening those who thought to avoid the tail by approaching the beast from the front. Those who were not swayed by the horns would certainly be made more than a bit weary by the jagged line of razors which lined the inside of the monster's mouth, dripping with acidic saliva. Upon each of the monster's feet were five long and sharp talons, capable of shredding a man beyond repair with a mere twitch. The beast roared, and those who heard saw the gates of the Underworld opening to welcome them. None with a shred of sanity would dare to approach this monster.

Sanity, of course, has no place in heroism.

"Pollux!" screamed a youthful man of sturdy build with long, blond hair, wielding a long sword. "Go for the belly! Slice the beast open!"

"You go for the belly, Castor," a nearly identical (disregarding his dark, braided hair and choice of weapon, his being a flail, rather than a sword) man screamed back. "I'm not getting anywhere near those claws!"

"You've gone soft," Castor ridiculed his brother. "There was a time when you would have raced me for the glory!"

With a quick jump to the side, Castor was able to block a tail strike with the broad side of his sword.

"Oh, I'll still race you," Pollux countered as he leaped out of the way of an attacking paw. "You'll just win this time!"

"I'd win anyway," Castor hollered back.

"Σκατά!" He dove toward the ground, avoiding the attacking jaws.

"Will you two shut up? Focus!" a dark, ruggedly handsome man reprimanded them. He was clothed with a breastplate, greaves, and a golden tunic, which hung across his torso.

He lunged for the creature's side with his own sword, only to be blocked by an intimidating talon. "Orpheus, any chance we'll get some music to soothe this thing soon?"

"I'm trying, Jason!" Orpheus, a thin and good-looking man with tawny hair and a soft face, answered. "This αηδιαστική σωρό από κοπριά broke the strings on my lyre! Give me a moment to fix them."

"Hurry it up!" Jason cried in desperation as he narrowly evaded a striking paw's talons.

The final member of the quintet, the largest and gruffest of the bunch, lunged with a grunt for the beast's tail. The serpent wriggled and lashed with rage as the hero seized it behind the head with his massive hand, paralyzing it momentarily. With his free hand, the hero crushed the serpent's head with a large rock. A small victory, only short-lived. The creature's back paw connected with the hero's torso, hurling him backward. Recovering, the hero sat up from the ground and groaned. The serpent was repairing itself and, within seconds, bellowed a wave of flame in the direction of the attacker. All the hero could do was drop to the ground and roll out of the way, the flames barely burning his back hair.

The beast rose to its back legs and let forth a monstrous roar, heard for many leagues. The heroes took this opportunity, whilst the beast was distracted, to regroup.

"Bravo, Hercules," Pollux chided the fifth hero. "You knew the tail would heal itself: It's a chimera! All you did was make it angry."

"You fared no better!" Hercules snapped back. "I have taught it the meaning of pain!"

"It doesn't seem to be taking the discovery very well," Orpheus muttered as he desperately tried to restring his lyre.

The beast returned to the ground and targeted the group of heroes. It lowered its horns as it prepared to charge.

"I have a plan!" Jason blurted out. He turned to Hercules. "Toss me onto the monster," he cried.

Hercules had no time to think with the beast thundering down upon them. As the group separated, diving out of the way of the beast's charge, Hercules took hold of Jason's tunic and tossed him into the air, toward the beast.

Jason's chest collided with the monster's shoulder, his breastplate protecting him from the majority of the impact. He gripped the chimera's mane and hung on as the monster thrashed and bucked, attempting to throw him loose. Quickly, Jason pulled himself up the chimera's back.

"Castor," Pollux cried, realizing Jason's plan, "the tail!"

Castor hefted his sword above his head and threw it with accuracy toward the tail, just as it began to rise toward Jason. The point of the blade pierced the serpent's neck, obstructing airflow.

Pollux, who had been charging the beast with his own weapon, froze. The serpent writhed about, attempting and failing to dislodge the sword. Turning, Pollux scowled at his brother. Castor's attack had effectively incapacitated the tail.

"I have your thanks." Castor smirked back at him. "And the glory."

"I should have sliced its belly open," Pollux muttered, frustrated.

Castor's quick action had allowed Jason time to get situated directly behind the creature's head. Once there, his mission was easy. Pulling the sword from his hip, Jason drove the weapon deep into the chimera's neck.

The beast paused for a moment as if unsure of what had just happened. It then wasted one of its last remaining breaths in an indignant roar as it threw its head back wrathfully. Jason used all of his might to hold on as the monster thrashed about, as if to avoid the obvious eventuality. As the monster raged, Jason withdrew his weapon, and plunged it into another area of the creature's exposed throat, just as deeply. The creature's blood ran thickly down his thighs and legs, splattering onto his chest and face as he withdrew the sword and repeated the strike in a third location.

With a final seizure, the beast whimpered. It then collapsed to its knees, and finally to the ground.

Jason slid down the beast's now-motionless back, dragging his weapon behind him. Landing upon the ground, he wiped his sword clean in the grass and retrieved Castor's blade from the now-motionless tail.

"We are victorious!" Hercules cheered as he ran to Jason. "Well done, brother!"

Jason barely had time to brace himself for Hercules' emphatic pat on the back. He stood again and smiled widely at his excited comrade.

"Argonauts forever!" Castor shouted with joy, his left fist in the air.

"Until the end!" Pollux continued the cheer, copying Castor's movement with his right fist.

The twins looked at each other and beat their testosterone-filled chests triumphantly.

"We are still Argonauts, are we?" Jason laughed. "Even without our ship?"

Orpheus looked away from his lyre momentarily. "People still tell our tales, and in those tales, we are the Argonauts," he said, smiling along with his comrades. "We've done great deeds, not soon to be forgotten. Besides, have we not just proven that we are still champions? I agree with Castor: Argonauts forever."

"To the end!" Castor and Pollux completed the cheer in unison, thrusting their opposing fists into the air once more.

Orpheus chuckled. "My point is made."

Jason laughed as he examined the group: Castor and Pollux, the Gemini twins, always opposing each other, while at the same time, complementing the other's talents with their own; Orpheus, the master musician, playing music on his lyre that could calm any beast; Hercules, the son of Zeus, mightiest of mortals and a god amongst heroes. Compared to his company, Jason felt almost inadequate. Still, wrapped around his breast was his own prize, the legendary Golden Fleece. The five of them were all that was left of the original Argonauts. Once their number had stood at nearly fifty. Time and war had worked their will, slowly eroding the group, chipping away at their numbers. Now, they were a mere shadow of the original cast. Still, as Jason looked at the small group, he felt a deep satisfaction. Perhaps they truly would be Argonauts forever.

II

He had been known as the man with one sandal.

It was not an impressive-sounding title (and a bit inaccurate, since most of the time, he wore two), but those who knew what it meant both respected and revered it.

Jason was the heir to the throne of Iolkos, placed in exile for his own safety when his cousin Pelias murdered his father, King Aeson, thus stealing the throne. During his ill-gotten reign, an Oracle warned Pelias that he would be murdered by a kinsman. The Oracle had also mentioned that he should be wary of anyone that he saw wearing only one sandal. From that day on, Pelias watched people's footwear very closely.

Jason spent the first twenty years of his life under the training of Chiron, the famous centaur who had also trained Hercules, in the mountains of Pelion. This was far enough away from Iolkos to avoid detection from Pelias, who surely would have killed Jason if he had known where Jason was. During this time, Jason had learned how to fight with as many weapons as Chiron knew of (including unarmed combat), how to survive in the wild, and how to ride and groom horses. Once he had reached the age of manhood Jason had set out to confront his cousin.

Just outside of Iolkos, there was a river. As Jason approached it, he saw an elderly woman sitting, looking forlorn. He asked her why she was so downcast. She informed Jason that she needed to cross the river, but there was no bridge for nearly a mile, and the water was moving too quickly for an old woman to wade across. She would surely drown. Jason volunteered to carry her across the river, and the woman accepted his help.

The river was indeed flowing quickly, and the bottom of the river was treacherous and dense with mud. Jason hefted the woman onto his back, secured her, and began to cross. About halfway through their journey, Jason's left foot snagged on something, and he kicked violently to get himself loose. He achieved his goal, and soon, both he and the woman were safely across.

Once on the other side, the old woman smiled and revealed herself to be the goddess Hera. She thanked Jason for his heroism and chivalry, promising to watch over him during his quest. Jason thanked the goddess and continued on his trek to Iolkos.

Upon reaching the town, Jason requested an audience with King Pelias. Perhaps his request came with great authority and confidence, or maybe Hera's blessing granted him favor that was evident to all, but he was uncharacteristically escorted directly into the throne room. There, he confronted the king without hesitation. Those within the throne room were amazed at the strange man's ferocity, his courage, and the learned way with which he spoke. Others were simply captivated by Jason's rippling musculature, his finely bronzed skin, and the golden curls that spun from his head to his shoulders.

King Pelias noticed none of this.

He was too distracted by Jason's barren left foot.

III

After the battle, the heroes separated, each going about their own life. Orpheus announced he was playing a show at a nearby tavern and, should any of them wish to join him, he could supply drinks at a discounted rate. While this tempted the Gemini brothers, they said that they also had a commitment back in Sparta with their wives, Phoebe and Hilaeira. Hercules was headed back to Olympus (plus, Orpheus' music always put him to sleep), so he could not make it. Jason honestly stated that he probably could have come, but he wanted instead to get home to his wife, Medea. She was surely waiting for him with a large meal. Thus, the company split, promising to meet again soon to see what adventures the world would hold.

Since Jason and Hercules both had destinations in the same direction, they walked together for a bit. Jason was still feeling pretty elated about the achievement, but Hercules seemed to walk with a cloud over his shoulders. They walked mostly in silence, occasionally engaging in petty small talk about the weather and local politics, topics that interested neither of them. The tension was too heavy.

"Hercules," Jason confronted him finally, "is something wrong?"

"No, no." Hercules shook his head unconvincingly. "It's nothing. Simply my own thoughts."

Jason shrugged and continued to walk beside his comrade.

Within a few steps, Hercules sighed.

"One chimera!" he blurted. "There was only one chimera, and it nearly bested us!"

Jason shook his head and chuckled, rolling his eyes at Hercules' unbridled ambition. "To be fair," he replied, "it was a rather large chimera."

"The size should not matter," Hercules grumbled. "We are the Argonauts. There should be no challenge too large for us. We should be defeating entire armies, not being paralyzed by a single beast. Remember the island of Lemnos?"

As Jason thought about the island, populated entirely by beautiful women, he smiled widely. "Of course I do." He laughed. "Although, I fail to see how eating good food, drinking the best wine, and receiving fine clothing could constitute a challenge."

"Those women had killed every other man that they had met," Hercules defended his assertion. "Yet, they did not kill the Argonauts."

"They did not even try!" Jason said, still happy with the memory. "I believe that they were simply overjoyed to see men once more. And if I might remind you," he continued, looking at Hercules with raised eyebrows, "I believe you abandoned us shortly after that when your armor bearer became drawn to that water nymph."

"Well, yes." Hercules dropped his gaze to the road sheepishly. "But, I came back, did I not? I am still an Argonaut, and that is my point. If we are Argonauts forever, then we should proclaim that."

Jason sighed as he considered reality. While his makeshift army of adventurers had at one time been a force to be reckoned with, it now seemed as if they were merely a dwindling cabal. There were those who still told of their adventures around campfires and sang of their journeys in taverns. They likely always would. However, the likelihood of new adventures seemed to be grow dimmer each day. The heroes left to find work elsewhere, or to live their quiet lives, free of adventure.

"Both of the Boreads are dead," Jason said, his face falling to his chest.

"I know," Hercules replied. "I was saddened when I learned of this. They were great warriors. That happens to adventurers sometimes. The risk of death comes with the territory."

"It does," Jason agreed, raising his head again to look Hercules in the eye. "Think, though: We are family men now, each with a wife to defend and care for. If I were to die on an adventure, who would care for Medea? I know that was Nestor's reason for leaving. He wanted to start a family, and he could not do that if his life were constantly in danger, as it was during his time with the Argonauts."

Hercules cocked an eyebrow. "Was that Euphemus' reasoning as well?"

Jason shook his head. "Euphemus chose to leave because politics offers a more stable salary than freelance adventuring. While you and I have our resources, not everyone else is so blessed. Some would find a steady pay more appealing, as Euphemus proved."

"He was weak." Hercules scowled. "Money is no substitute for adventure."

"Oh," Jason chuckled. "Should I tell Aigio's mayor to keep our fee?"

Hercules swatted Jason on the back of the head. "That is not the point. We are adventurers, we are champions, and above all, we are Argonauts. Argonauts forever!"

With his fist thrust into the air, Hercules looked expectantly toward Jason for the completed cheer. Jason looked back at him with regretful eyes.

"There are but five of us now." Jason sighed.

"So, maybe we should recruit more members."

"Maybe we should let go of the dream."

Hercules stopped walking abruptly. Jason walked two steps more, then turned to see his comrade glaring down at him darkly.

"I only stated what needed to be said," Jason defended himself.

Hercules' scowl deepened. Jason imagined he might see steam escaping from his ears and fire about to launch from his eyes.

"You still wear that Fleece," Hercules growled.

Jason paused and ran his fingers through the golden fibers that composed his makeshift tunic. He understood Hercules' accusation. While Jason was suggesting that perhaps they stop attempting to be heroes, his legacy was still wrapped around his chest, rather than hanging on a wall in his chamber or on display in a trophy case at his dwelling. While the thought of peace and tranquility appealed to him, the thought of taking off the Fleece nearly caused him physical pain. There was still adventure left in Jason and, until that spirit was quieted, he would not be able to simply let the Argonauts pass away.

"All right." Jason stepped back to where Hercules was standing. "I'm in. What are you proposing?"

Hercules smiled, victorious once again. "Well, like you said, five champions are not enough. We should recruit others. I think that we should form a list of possible candidates and proceed with that accordingly. There are plenty of eligible heroes who would be over-joyed to join our ranks."

"I agree." Jason smiled, becoming more excited about the prospect as they continued the discussion. "Shall we go to the tavern where Orpheus is playing in order to discuss this further?"

"No." Hercules shook his head. "I wouldn't be able to pay atten-tion, what with the falling to sleep and all. Let us go to Oblivion."

"Oh!" Jason's grin widened, excitedly. "I've heard of Oblivion! That's definitely where we should go."

"Argonauts forever!" Hercules repeated his unanswered cheer with his fist in the air once more.

"To the end!" Jason replied this time, punching the air as was the accepted custom.

The champions left the road on which they had been traveling and proceeded instead down a detoured path, toward the future.

IV

Hercules made his way back to the table where Jason was seated, carrying two large glass goblets filled to the brim with a dark bever-age, topped with a thick head of foam. The tavern was dimly lit with a soft light provided by candles situated strategically around the room and by lanterns hung on the walls. Creatures and deities from all different regions sat basking in the ambiance of the tavern and enjoying their drinks.

On one end of the room, there was a long bar, where two attrac-tive women served drinks to patrons perched on stools. Opposite the bar, there was a small stage where an acting troupe was preparing for the evening show. At one table, the god Anubis could be seen discussing the afterlife with Nanna, the Norse goddess of grief. Elsewhere, Jason spotted Narcissus, sitting proudly with a wide smile and a beautiful water nymph on his arm. Drinking alone in a corner sat the tentacled Cthulhu, a god whom none of the others really understood. For his part, it did not seem he desired to be understood. He was satisfied sitting alone, drinking his beer, and dreaming of worlds to devour.

The bartending god Dionysus walked through the tavern, moving from table to table, making small talk with the patrons. He laughed at jokes, whether funny or not, and refilled drinks from the pitcher he carried with him. This was his tavern, and all were welcome, providing that they did not make too much of a scene. If they did make a scene, it had better be an entertaining one, otherwise they would be thrown out. The occasional fight could not be avoided, but if it was a foolish quarrel or a one-sided combat, the value was seriously diminished.

Hercules sat down in his seat, considered the drinks closely for a moment, and then passed the one with a thicker head to Jason. Jason accepted it and drank deeply. He made a face as he swallowed the fluid.

"Ugh," he complained. "This is not wine."

"It's beer," Hercules explained. "It's a drink that we got from Egypt, Mesopotamia, or some other culture we conquered." Hercules lifted his own goblet to his lips and drank.

He belched.

"It's good," the demigod continued. "It probably cures some disease or something, but even if it doesn't, I like it. I think it's kind of like what the Egyptians used to give the slaves when they were working."

"Was it a punishment?" Jason stared into his cup. "Because, I have to say, it tastes like punishment."

"You have to get used to it." Hercules took another draw. "Once you are, you'll love it. I can't get enough of this stuff now."

Jason took another sip of his beer and cringed as he swallowed.

"So, explain to me how time works here again?" he inquired. "It stops, right?"

Hercules nodded his head and lowered his mug. "I guess so," he said. "Time stops while you're here. It's a separate reality. Dionysus promised Dad that he would provide the best wine to Olympus if Dad were able to get him a bar where the patrons would never have to leave. It doesn't work right, though, because time keeps moving in the world outside. So, you could be here for what feels like an hour, step back into the world, and find out that you've been gone for a couple days."

"Is that not somewhat dangerous?" Jason frowned. "I mean, how can you tell if you've been gone too long?"

"Oh, don't worry about that." Hercules dismissed the concern with a wave. "The most that I have ever been here was a week. What is the worst that could happen? Are you afraid that your wife is going to leave you?"

Jason shook his head. "No," he said. "Medea and I are very committed to each other."

"Then don't worry about it." Hercules took another large swallow from his drink and rendered another large burp. "Just drink your beer."

Jason took another sip, a bit larger than the last. "So, while you're here at the bar," Jason swallowed with a cringe, "would you age?"

"No." Hercules shook his head. "That was the whole point. Oblivion is an escape from everything, even time."

"That is nice." Jason smiled widely.

Hercules spread his arms wide, indicating the entire room. "Why do you think it's so popular?" he asked, beaming.

"Well, it's certainly not because of beer." Jason took another drink. "Now, let's get down to business. Who is the first hero that you'd want as an Argonaut?"

"Odysseus," Hercules stated. "He's strong, courageous, and plus, he knows how to captain a ship. If we were to revive the Argos, he would be a perfect crew member."

Jason shook his head. "I agree that he would be perfect," he said. "In fact, I agree so much that I asked him to join the Argonauts after Troy fell. He told me on no uncertain terms that he was not interested. All he wanted to do was get home to his wife in Ithaca."

"Troy fell a long time ago, Jason." Hercules raised his eyebrows. "Maybe his desire has changed."

"Perhaps." Jason shrugged. "Still, I don't think we should count on him joining. What of Achilles? He was a great warrior, and instrumental in the Trojan war."

Hercules rolled his eyes. "The man all but died," he exclaimed, "just from being stabbed in the heel!"

"Yet, that is his only vulnerable spot," Jason insisted. "If it becomes an issue, we could simply get him better sandals!"

"Everyone knows of the spot now, though," Hercules continued his critique. "That makes him a liability. I certainly would not be comfortable with him having my back. Now, Perseus, that would be someone I could get behind."

"Oh, Perseus would be great," Jason agreed. "Plus, he rides Pegasus, and that would be an added resource. Do you know where he is now?"

"Absolutely." Hercules nodded, eagerly. "He's the founder and ruler of Mycenae, so that's probably where he is."

"He's a politician?" Jason grimaced.

"Oh." Hercules' glee dropped with his gaze. "Right. Well, we can still ask."

"What about Atalanta?" Jason asked.

"No!" Hercules declared emphatically. "No women!"

"She is a good fighter," Jason insisted. "She bested Peleus in the funeral games back when my cousin was ruling my country. Plus, who can forget the Calydonian boar hunt? She was great as an Argonaut. I do not see a reason why she would not join us again."

"Perhaps," Hercules relented. "I still do not like it, though. In my experience, women warriors always seem to cause strife. Besides, none of them seem to like me."

"Did you not get beaten up by the Amazons a couple times?" Jason chuckled.

"Maybe." Hercules shifted his eyes. "But that was different. There were ... a lot of them."

"Well, I suppose that would be a good excuse," Jason laughed loudly, "for anyone but you."

Hercules paused and took another long drink from his goblet. He looked to Jason, seriously. "This is going to take a bit of time, isn't it?"

"Good evening, gentlemen," came a cheerful voice. Looking up, Jason saw the welcoming face of their host as he approached them with a pitcher full of beer. He wore his usual casual smile, his dark hair combed back, away from his forehead. His eyes sparkled with life as he stopped at their table.

"How are things going tonight?" he asked, the smile never flickering.

"Hail, Dionysus," Jason returned the greeting with a smile of his own. "The place looks terrific."

"Thank you, Jason." Dionysus laughed. "It's not much, but I do what I can. What are you boys doing this evening?"

"We're recruiting more Argonauts," Hercules informed him. "Well, technically, we're just finding candidates, but after that, we're going to start recruiting."

"So, the Argonauts are returning." Dionysus raised his eyebrows as he tipped his pitcher in order to refill Hercules' glass. "I'm looking forward to hearing of your new ventures. Once you've formed this new crew, won't you bring them here so I may meet them? The first round is on me."

"We never went away, Dionysus," Hercules insisted. "In fact, we just finished slaying a chimera. You should have seen this thing, Dion! It was huge, like, twenty feet long. It breathed fire from its tail, and its teeth were like swords. We barely survived!"

"Wow." Dionysus took a step backward, looking impressed. "That does sound like a story. I cannot wait to hear it. Sadly, I must be getting back to my duties now." Dionysus put a melodramatic hand to his forehead. "Oh, so much work, it never stops, never stops." He sighed with exaggerated exhaustion.

Jason and Hercules both laughed at the act.

"It was good to see you boys." Dionysus smiled authentically. He then motioned to the stage. "I hope your work does not prevent you from enjoying the show."

"There's a show tonight?" Hercules turned toward the stage, where a satyr sat prepping himself next to a wood nymph. Across the stage, a man was fitting himself into a gorgon outfit.

"Oh wow!" Hercules exclaimed. "Is that really Pan?"

Dionysus chuckled and winked at Hercules. "It is indeed, brother. Enjoy the show."

Turning his back to the table, Dionysus walked back to the bar, stopping to wipe off an empty table en route.

"Check it out, Jason!" Hercules pointed excitedly to the stage. "It's Pan!"

"I see that." Jason smiled. "But now, I think we should really get back to the project at hand."

"Yeah, yeah, we will." Hercules' eyes never deviated from the stage. "We'll do that right after the show."

"If we are wanting to become a presence again, I think—"

"Shush." Hercules turned to Jason, holding his finger to his lips. "It's starting."

Jason started to become concerned. "Hercules," he said, "I really should not be gone that long."

Hercules did not respond, but four or five neighboring tables shushed Jason for him. As the lights in the tavern dimmed and music began to play, Jason sighed and shook his head. It seemed that he had lost this battle, but it was only one show. It was Pan, after all. What harm could one show do? Jason sat back and lifted the beer to his lips again.

The stuff really was not all that bad, once you got used to it.

Dionysus looked back to where the two were seated and smiled slyly to himself. It was rare that he found two such popular heroes in his bar together, especially ones with virtually endless resources. Even if they could not afford their tab at the end of their stay, Dionysus knew that Zeus, Hercules' father, would never allow his favorite son to be indebted to the establishment.

At that moment, Dionysus began to contrive a plan to keep them at Oblivion for as long as he could.

V

Hera had never liked Hercules.

Hercules was the son of Zeus and Alcmene, a mortal woman. While this was not the first of Zeus' affairs, Alcmene was beneath the standards that Hera had set, even for Zeus' extramarital conquests. Gods, after all, are almost expected to sleep around. Hera herself, the goddess of marriage, had gotten into her own share of affairs. Alcmene, however, was unworthy. Her illegitimate child was therefore unworthy as well.

When Hercules was still a supposedly defenseless infant, Hera made an attempt to eliminate him. She set two venomous serpents loose in his crib. To this end, Hercules first showed his inhuman strength. Taking a serpent in each hand, he strangled them both. Whether this was intentional or simply an infant's attempt at exercising newly found muscles is not known. Later, when his nurse came in to check on him, she found Hercules playing with the two dead snakes as if they were toys.

Through his youth, Hercules had little influence from the gods. He grew to be a healthy young man, having the strength of ten others. Alcmene's human husband, Amphitryon, adopted and raised Hercules as if he were his own. He received no special treatment, either positive or negative, through his youth. Amphitryon was a farmer, and one day he sent Hercules to tend to the cattle. Hercules herded the cattle onto the side of a mountain nearby his home. As the cattle grazed, young Hercules noticed two beautiful women approaching him. These women were actually nymphs. They introduced themselves to Hercules as Pleasure and Virtue, informing him that they each had an offer for him. With her long, blond hair flowing behind her, Pleasure grew close to Hercules, running her nimble fingers through his hair and down his back. Rubbing her perfect body against his own, Pleasure kissed him gently on his neck, again on his cheek, and again behind his ear, nibbling gently upon his earlobe. Her breath smelled of sweet honey as she made her offer: a pleasant and easy life, but without adventure and satisfaction.

The second nymph, Virtue, made no attempt to seduce Hercules. Whilst Pleasure continued to lavish herself on the young man, Virtue, with her strong body and auburn hair, stood her ground. She simply smiled at Hercules and offered a severe but glorious life. It would be more difficult than he could ever anticipate, but he would be remembered for decades, even centuries, afterward. He would work for every glory he achieved, but because of this, each glory would truly be his own.

Hercules considered the choice that was presented to him. The offer of a pleasant and easy life was tempting, surely. It was also difficult to think of anything else, with the Pleasure nymph enrapturing him with her stimulation. Still, his earthly father had taught him the value of hard work. He had taught Hercules that hard work was its own reward, and that it would bring forth profit. A man who achieves a world of riches through the sweat of another is not a man at all. To truly know the value of something, one must first earn it.

With Pleasure's arms still strung about his neck, Hercules locked eyes with Virtue and accepted her offer. Repulsed, Pleasure abandoned Hercules immediately, while Virtue stepped up to replace her. She smiled at the young man lovingly, and pulled his body close to her own in a tight embrace. Bringing her lips to his, she kissed him deeply. Hercules closed his eyes as her tongue filled his mouth. She did not taste or smell as sweetly as Pleasure had, but she was real and authentic. His saliva mixed with hers, and Hercules knew that he would never regret the choice he made. The kiss lasted for what felt like hours, and after it was through, Hercules opened his eyes to find that he was alone with the cattle once more. He could still feel Virtue's breath inside of him.

Throughout this entirety, Hera watched him and waited for her moment.

Meanwhile, at Oblivion...

Over the years, Dionysus had watched Cupid evolve from Aphrodite's upstart, practically useless, son to the fashionable, worldly character that he was now. Over the years, very few had lost as much as he. Now, as he approached the bartender with a cigar in one hand and a glass of wine in the other, he looked confident and secure. Dionysus was almost proud of him! He had never seen one recover from their woes so elegantly as he had.

From the look in his eyes right now, though, Dionysus knew what was coming. It was not as though he hadn't dealt with the problem many times before over the past hundred years or so.

"Hello Eros." He smiled, using Cupid's original name, hoping to take him off guard. "How are you? How's the drink treating you tonight?"

Cupid didn't skip a beat. Instead, he pointed at a table in the center of the room.

"Is that," he began haltingly, "both Jason and Hercules over there, drinking beer as if they haven't a care in the world?"

"Why, yes, I believe it is," Dionysus confirmed, his smile never flickering. "I hadn't noticed! I wonder how long they've been here."

Cupid's jaw dropped. "How long they've—" he began to stammer in exasperation. "Zeus has been searching for— They have been— The war—!"

"Hmm." Dionysus nodded, furrowing his brow with false concern. "Yes, I suppose they would have been useful in the war. It's a shame that they were not here during that time; I would have alerted them, regarding the conflict, for sure. Ah, well; one cannot change the past. Isn't it funny that, with as many powers as we Olympians have, changing the past is not amongst them? Maybe we should look into that one."

Cupid's eyes bulged with rage. "My mother died!" he blurted out angrily.

"Keep your voice down," Dionysus said, frowning at him. "This is a place of relaxation. I can't have you disturbing that."

Cupid shook his head vigorously, attempting to organize his thoughts. "I have to tell Zeus," he muttered, turning away from Dionysus, toward the exit.

"I agree," Dionysus said. "Just pay your tab, and you can be on your way."

"Oh." Cupid turned back. "Right, my tab. Can you ring me out, please?"

Dionysus signaled a maenad on the other end of the bar and pointed to Cupid. "Right then, we'll have that right up for you," he said, returning his attention to Cupid. "While you wait, let me freshen your drink, on the house."

"O...kay..." Cupid frowned at Dionysus' uncharacteristic generosity, but handed him the glass, just the same. "Yeah, that sounds nice. I guess one last drink can't hurt."

"Not at all," Dionysus said, his smile returning. "I just got something special in that I think you'll like. It's a wonderful blend; you'll forget all of your troubles."

He smiled as he filled Cupid's glass again, complete with his own "special ingredient." He was not worried about the threatened report to Zeus. He had, after all, been doing this for a very long time. Well, perhaps it would be considered a long time, in any place but Oblivion.

22

VI

It was a beautiful day, just as it was every day. The sun shone brightly in the pure blue sky where big, puffy, white clouds hung like decorations. The air was clean, and the temperature was comfortably warm. The morning frost that had nourished the ground was quickly drying on the grass of the field, just between Oblivion and the dimensional nexus, which lead back to Earth. The Field of Sobriety, Dionysus called it. It stretched for nearly a mile. No animals made a habitat there. There were no trees or foliage of any kind. No birds sang in the sky, and no wind rustled the grass. It was simply a field for the guests of Oblivion to walk through, while preparing themselves to enter the world again. What occurs at Oblivion stays at Oblivion, including the drunkenness.

If one were to listen to the field, they would hear singing. Not birdsong of any sort, since there are no birds within the field, but singing still. The song was not pleasant to listen to, nor did it make any sort of sense in classic music theory. Still, it was music, in a sense. It was the type of music that one can only hear when two drunken men attempt to sing a song, when they can neither remember the words nor the tune.

After three attempts, the song was abandoned, concluded with an encore of laughter.

One of the men tripped over a root that was not there, and the other attempted to bend over, in order to help him up again. Both actions were failures, and both men wound up on the ground, laughing.

"My," Jason declared as he rose unsteadily to his feet. "Oh my! That bar, you know, that bar was great!"

"Oblivion," Hercules declared with as proper a voice as he could manage in his current state of inebriation. He crawled to his feet before continuing his advertisement. "The time where bar stops. Time stops, yeah, time stops. Where it's always happy hour, but the drinks are never half off."

"Unless you're the bartender's nephew." Jason laughed loudly.

"No, no." Hercules threw a wavering finger in Jason's face. "Dionysus, he's not my uncle. He's, I think he's my stepbrother. Yeah, step-brother, twice removed, or something... I dunno..."

"Women sleep with your dad a lot," Jason said. "And they're always different women. I think your dad's easy."

"You take that back," Hercules commanded Jason with the same unsteady finger, stepping a bit closer to get in Jason's face. "My father, he is not easy. Girls just... I mean, women just... he's just popular, okay? You wish that you could have as much sex as he does."

"All of Sparta combined wishes they could have as much sex as he does," Jason replied, not backing down. "Your dad, he has a lot of sex. And it's always with different women!"

"Oh, yeah?" Hercules bent his face into Jason's own. "Is that what you think? Well... well, you stink! You couldn't have sex with anything right now, you stink so bad. That fleece that you wear, the golden one? It stinks."

"Is that so?" Jason sneered. "Well... you need to wash your hair! You need to wash your hair because your hair is gross."

"No!" Hercules threw his head back triumphantly. "For the gods have decreed that I shall lose my strength if I wash my hair. I must never wash my hair!"

"What?" Jason looked at Hercules suspiciously. "When did this happen?"

"While you were in the washroom a little bit ago," Hercules answered.

The two of them locked eyes and stared each other down for a moment. Jason broke first with a snort, then Hercules with a barely concealed laugh. Soon, they were both laughing hard enough to hurt their sides.

"All right," Jason struggled to say. "All right, we've been walking for a long time now. When do you think that we'll—"

"Γαμώτο!" Jason suddenly screamed and stop dead in his tracks.

Hercules, walking a few paces behind him, stopped as well. He looked at Jason, drunkenly. "What are you screaming for? You were just walking, then you stopped and screamed."

Jason paused for a moment. He stood up straight and looked down at his hands. They were still there, as were his feet and torso. Jason ran his ten fingers through his hair (which was still there, apparently) and turned to Hercules in shock and horror.

"Hercules," he said, fearfully. "I'm sober."

"Oh," Hercules sighed, sympathetically. "I'm sorry, brother."

"Hours, maybe days of drinking, and now I'm completely sober!"

"Yeah." Hercules stumbled forward until he was standing next to Jason. At that point, his demeanor completely changed. He stood up straight, dusted himself off, and looked at Jason through a completely sober pair of eyes.

"That happens at Oblivion," he explained. "Dionysus thought it would be easier to explain long absences, sometimes days or even weeks, if the explainer was not drunk. Plus, he didn't want them to go accidentally blurting out details about Oblivion to common men. It's still a fairly elite club, after all. So, Dionysus set the Field of Sobriety right outside. No matter how drunk you are when you enter the field, you are always sober when you reach the other side."

Jason looked back at the field with dismay. "Couldn't we have stayed in the field a little while longer?"

Hercules laughed and patted Jason on the shoulder. "Nah," he said. "We've probably been gone too long already. I don't even remember why we came here in the first place, now!"

"We were drafting more Argonauts," Jason reminded him. "We didn't actually get it done, though."

"That's all right." Hercules chuckled. "There'll be plenty of time for that in the future."

He reached out his hand and felt for the barrier between worlds. The air around his hand shimmered and crinkled like transparent foil. Hercules smiled at Jason.

"Are you ready to get back to the real world?" he asked.

Jason shrugged. "I suppose I must be," he said reluctantly. "How long do you think we were actually out of commission?"

Hercules shook his head and laughed. "Probably too long," he said. "A few months, perhaps. Maybe even a year."

"Medea's not going to be happy with me." Jason laughed.

"No, she's not," Hercules agreed, jokingly. "It's okay, though. We're legends, we can find new women."

"You, maybe. I happen to love my wife." Jason motioned toward the portal. "Shall we?"

"After you." Hercules graciously stepped aside, waving for Jason to proceed. "I wonder how the world has changed since we've been gone."

Jason wondered this as well as the two of them stepped across the barrier.

VII

As the legends emerged on the other side of the nexus, they stepped into an alien world. Hercules froze as he looked around. Monstrous edifices, taller than any that he had ever imagined, reached into the sky, covered with what appeared to be eyes. Horrid monsters raced past him, growling loudly, with their eyes blazing. Within the body of each beast, Hercules could see the humans each had devoured, still alive and most looking quite unhappy to be so. To Hercules' right, there was a strange building, beside which there was a long line of monstrosities. One after the other, they would bring themselves up to a projection. The projection would open, and a human holding a bag or a tray would partially emerge, handing the objects to the monsters, or rather to the humans that the monsters had consumed. Hercules watched in shock as he saw one of the humans begin to consume what had been handed to them. This must be how the beasts kept their human slaves alive.

Jason witnessed the horror as well. Humans dressed in strange, tight, and restricting clothing walked past him, some looking his direction as if he were the freak. Some of these humans seemed to be speaking into strange looking shells, holding one end to their ear, and the other to their mouth. A few yards in front of them was a strange, square building, surrounded by several boxes from which hoses spewed. Jason watched in horror as the beasts would stop next to these boxes, and regurgitate their human victims. The humans would then take hold of the hose and place it within the beast's body. They then waited until the beast had taken its fill, then replaced the hose and allowed the beast to consume them once again.

The odors in this place were disgusting and offensive. Hercules could not identify even one of them, but none of them were pleasant. Even the humans who walked past them smelled grotesque. Should the odor they emitted not be as foul, they smelled as if they were trying to cover their stench with less offensive scents. However, the scents that they chose were almost as offensive as the humans themselves. This was nothing, however, compared to the stomach-churning clouds that were emitted from the beasts. As they roared back and forth, a cloud of unearthly stench followed them, polluting the air; Hercules' stomach churned.

One of the humans took notice of Jason. He stopped talking into his shell and smiled, babbling something in a language that neither Jason nor Hercules understood.[1]

Jason stared back at him, mystified.

The stranger's smile faded. He continued babbling, this time slower and louder.[2]

Jason shrugged, having no idea how to answer the stranger.

The man uttered a final frustrated phrase before returning to his shell.[3]

Jason watched as he walked off. There was nothing he could have done. He remembered how the Romans would take those who spewed such nonsense and throw them to the lions.

Distracted by the sensations, Hercules absentmindedly stepped into the path of one of the beasts. The beast screamed as it stopped directly in front of him and began to roar its challenge at him.

Hercules was never one to back down from a fight. Turning to the beast, he raised his fists to his shoulders and smashed them both into the front of the monster. To his surprise, it crumbled with ease, displaying the creature's interior. The human prisoner freed himself and ran from the scene, screaming. Hercules assumed that he was screaming with joy, but the human never stopped to thank him or offer him his daughter as payment for his heroism. Perhaps he were so overjoyed to finally be free of the beast that he merely forgot. Hercules proceeded to destroy the beast's inner organs, becoming covered in the creature's foul black blood.

"Hercules!" Jason screamed after watching the champion in battle. "What is this place?"

"Come, Jason!" Hercules turned to his comrade. "Let us free the humans from these monsters! Argonauts forever!"

"To the end!" Jason answered.

Thus, the two of them ran out into battle to destroy as many of the beasts as they could.

CHAPTER TWO

I

ZEUS LOVED MORNINGS. EACH DAY PRESENTED NEW opportunities and another chance to resurrect the glory that had been stripped from him more than two thousand years ago.

The transition from the Greek Empire to the Roman Empire had not been difficult. When the Romans had come into dominion, replacing the Greeks, they had accepted the Greek pantheon as their own. They had given most of the gods new names, but had essentially left the stories and legacies alone. Historians had theorized that Rome had done this simply because their own gods were silly or incompetent. Zeus knew better. Rome had no gods. No gods had sought their worship. The Romans had been a war-driven, savage, and unimaginative people.

This was one of the main reasons that Zeus had never fully implemented Jupiter, the name Rome had given him, as his own.

When Rome replaced Greece as the dominant powerhouse in the world, transference of the pantheon made sense. After all, gods needed to go to where the power was. Most of the Olympians, and the others associated with them, continued to use their Greek names. They accepted that they could be worshiped under both. Eros was really the only one that dismissed his Greek name almost completely. Zeus felt that the name Cupid didn't have the same dignity, but it hadn't been his choice to make.

The world moved away from Rome. The power shifted, and problems arose. The world expanded, and as it did, different cultures began to interact. These groups of people had their own gods. The Greeks had always gotten along with, or at least tolerated, other pantheons before, such as Egyptian and Babylonian. These new gods did not seem willing to simply co-exist. Many of them wanted sole dominion over certain territories. Some even argued that there should be no other pantheons, save their own. A great war began, which made Ares happy, but it made everyone else concerned, or worse, endangered. The outcome of the war did not turn in the Olympians' favor. Zeus and the others saw their time in Earth's reality had ended. Through the aid of a portal Hephaestus had built, Zeus and the others moved all of Olympus (plus a few other significant sites of power) into another dimension, existing parallel to Earth, with the same parameters and physical laws. This is where they had existed since that time, with the exception of Aphrodite. Her fate was much more tragic.

From his dimension, Zeus was able to watch the Earth and study the events that occurred there. As he watched, he noticed the other pantheons growing weaker, some all but disappearing completely, while his own was remembered and often studied. This brought him hope that one day, the Greek/Roman pantheon would be able to return to the Earth, reasserting their power and their strength. This hope dwindled as time passed. Now it was nearly dead. Zeus wondered if he even wanted to return to Earth. He was beginning to wonder if he even wanted to be a god any longer.

Humans no longer seemed to worship gods. They seemed to worship other things, such as money, technology, entertainment, and youth. Returning to Earth might be a fruitless venture. Still, Zeus watched Earth closely, even walking it now and then in the guise of a human. There must be something that he was missing.

The morning routine had always irritated him. One would think that a god could simply say, "Be clean and refreshed." and *POOF* they would be. This was not the case.

Each day, Zeus had to get up, shower, shave, put on deodorant, trim his fingernails, blow his nose, and all those other human things. It was one of the parameters of this new dimension that Hephaestus had found for them, and it was obnoxious. It was, however, what needed to happen. He had tried not doing it for a time. That lasted about a week. Hera complained about the smell after the second day. She was always complaining about something or other, so Zeus had not paid as much attention. By day five, the other gods began to display adverse reactions, coughing to suppress a gag or turning away from him. By the end of the week, even Zeus was disgusted by his own smell. Hera was extremely appreciative when he emerged, smelling like the king of gods again.

He had shaved his beard some time ago. When he had done it, he had justified it as a simple need for change. He had worn the beard for a very long time, after all. Zeus had intended to grow it back. Looking at himself in the mirror, he found he looked much younger, and this pleased him. Hera was equally as pleased, and she seemed to enjoy kissing his bare face more than she ever had with the beard. Thus, shaving was added to the daily bath chamber dance.

As Zeus ran the razor down his chin, removing the stubble, he considered relegating the task to every-other-day.

A hurried knocking on the chamber door made him jump, and as a small spot of blood appeared from where he had nicked himself, Zeus finalized the decision.

Picking up a washrag and wiping away the spot, he answered the knocking. "I'll just be a moment," he called to the knocker.

"Zeus," came the frantic voice of Hermes. "Something has just happened that... well, it's something that you might..."

From the other side of the door, Zeus could hear Hermes taking a breath and settling himself. "Sir," he said in a much calmer voice. "I think that we might have a problem."

"I'll be out in a moment, Hermes," Zeus answered, not moved by Hermes' panic at all. "I'm shaving."

"Sir, this is something that you're going to want to see immediately."

Zeus sighed heavily and pulled his bathrobe tightly around himself. He opened the door and smiled as broadly and sarcastically as he could.

"Good morning, Hermes," he said with false and exaggerated cheer to the thin, dark-haired man that stood on the other side. "How are you today?"

"This really isn't the time for..." Hermes stopped himself. "Good morning, Zeus," he started again, attempting to remain calm. "I'm fine, thank you. How are you?"

"I'm not doing too well right now." Zeus frowned and pointed to where the speck of blood had reemerged. "I cut myself shaving."

"I see that, sir," Hermes continued. Standing there next to Zeus in a bathrobe, he looked very out of place in his dark suit and designer shoes. Hermes had never truly learned how to relax. "I'm afraid that my news probably isn't going to improve your morning much."

Zeus rolled his eyes. "What's going on?" he asked. Hermes always seemed on the verge of a nervous breakdown, so Zeus was not very impressed by this display.

"Well," Hermes began, choosing his words very carefully. "I suppose that the upside is that we've found Hercules."

"What?" Zeus' face exploded with glee. He had been searching for his son for over two thousand years. Zeus could think of no better news.

"That is great news!" he cheered, placing enthusiastic hands on Hermes' shoulders. "How can you say that this is anything but..."

The instant ecstasy that he had felt at the announcement began to fade. The world had changed a lot in two thousand years.

Zeus leveled a very sober look into Hermes. "What did he do?"

. . .

This is James Novus, coming to you with a breaking news story. Chaos has ensued on Prospect Avenue, close to downtown Cleveland today. Two men, dressed as gladiators, appeared suddenly in the streets and began to attack commuters. Actually, they don't seem to be attacking the people, so much as the people's cars. The police have arrived on the scene, and have taken control of the situation. We take you now to reporter Candace Amentia, live at the scene. What can you tell us about the situation, Candace?

Well, James, saying that the police have control of the situation is a bit of an overstatement. It's true that they have the two men at gunpoint right now, but they do not appear to be giving up quite yet. The larger of the two is holding a door from one of the destroyed cars, and he seems to be treating it as if it were a shield. The police continue to attempt communication with these savages, but they don't appear to speak English, and communicate only with each other, using an unknown language. The police have not opened fire yet, but if communication continues to be impossible, it may become necessary. The men destroyed three cars, two SUVs, and a truck before the police arrived. As you can see behind me, the men do not seem to be exhausted at all. This could be evidence that the men are on a performance-enhancing drug.

Thank you for the update, Candace. We'll continue to keep you posted as the situation unfolds. In another story, a local celebrity turns thirty-five today, but with the amount of plastic surgery that she's had, she thinks she should only be considered thirty-two. As strange as that may sound to us, this celebrity is pursuing a court order to have her birth certificate reprinted...

II

Zeus watched the scene in horror. There stood his son, dirty and filthy, as if he had not bathed in centuries, wielding a car door as if it were a trophy. The human enforcements had their modern weapons pointed at him, prepared to terminate his life if he refused to cooperate soon. Standing behind Hercules was another man, appearing only slightly more confused than he.

"Who is that?" Zeus pointed to the man.

"That's Jason of Iolkos," Hera answered, also viewing the scene. "He was the one that retrieved the Golden Fleece, remember?"

"Yes," Zeus confirmed. "I see it tied across his chest."

"He was no doubt caught up in one of your son's idiotic schemes," Hera sneered.

Zeus was about to contradict her, but from the looks of what was happening, she could be correct.

"What are they doing?" roared a large man. He had the physique of a bodybuilder, wore a chest plate, bracers, greaves, and a large helmet. "They appeared out of nowhere, completely demolished six motor vehicles, and now they're standing off against those silly humans and their guns! What were they thinking? And, why did I not do that years ago?"

"Because we are not at war with the mortals, Ares," a beautiful woman informed him. She had white hair and dressed in a flowing silver dress, with a beautiful crescent moon pendant around her neck.

"That's not my fault!" Ares returned.

Hera let her head sink into her hands. "I always knew that something like this would happen," she muttered. "I told you that this would happen, didn't I?" she asked, looking up at Zeus.

"Really, love?" Zeus glared back at her, keeping his rage at bay. "You really told me that Hercules would suddenly appear in the middle of modern humanity and disrupt society like this? You told me that? Because that's a conversation I think I'd remember!"

"What I have said is that he's irresponsible," Hera huffed. "He's unpredictable and irrational, as demonstrated by this fiasco. He always has been, and—"

"—and you let him marry your daughter!" Zeus lashed back, feeling the anger in his throat.

"Do you really want to bring that up?" Hera moved her queen into checkmate position. "My daughter is dead because of him!"

Had they been playing chess, Zeus would have just watched Hera, placing his king in checkmate. The two simply glared at each other for a moment until the moon goddess broke the silence.

"Oh look," Artemis pointed to the scene. "Bullets can't hurt him."

The police had given up trying to negotiate, and had opened fire. The door repelled most of the bullets, but the ones that did connect with Hercules' chest simply left large red welts.

"Of course they don't hurt him," Ares sneered. "He's a god, after all."

"He's only half god, Ares dear," Hera corrected him. "Don't forget that his mother was that human slut, Alcmene."

"Oh, give me break!" Zeus threw his hands up into the air. "I sleep around with a mortal woman, and now I have to hear about it forever? It was only one time!"

Four heads turned to him suspiciously. Artemis actually laughed.

"Well," Zeus shuffled his feet, "it was only one time with her. And it's not like all of you haven't had affairs!"

"What part of 'virgin goddess' do you not understand?" Artemis asked.

"Virgin," Ares scoffed. "I heard about you and that Orion guy."

Artemis punched Ares in the jaw. "We were just friends!" she cried. "We both liked hunting, and that was all! Can't a woman have male friends without getting accused of sleeping with them?"

"I don't know," Hera replied. "Ask you father."

Zeus squared his jaw and turned to his wife. He would have had a biting response (really; he was just about to think of it) but Hermes' hand on his shoulder stopped him.

Hermes motioned toward the scene where things were rapidly

escalating. "You should probably do something about this, big guy," he told Zeus.

Zeus swallowed his pride and sighed. "You're right," he nodded. "I'll be back."

With a sigh, Zeus began to walk toward the portal between realities.

III

The pebbles that these men were launching at him felt like massive bee strings. Hercules protected Jason, whose skin was much more vulnerable, by placing himself between the attackers and Jason.

They had destroyed six of the monsters, rescuing the devoured humans, before the first of the counterattacks. At first, it was difficult to determine that it was an attack, since it just appeared to be a group of angry humans pointing metallic sticks at them and shouting in that strange tongue the humans of this place used. Then, the sticks produced a loud banging noise and launched tiny pebbles at them with great speed. Each one that hit his chest burned for a moment before dropping to the ground, leaving behind a stinging red welt. These were minor injuries that did not bother Hercules all that much. They were, however, still irritating. He was becoming annoyed.

"These people don't seem appreciate our help," Hercules said to Jason.

"Well, I certainly appreciate you right now," Jason replied from where he stood, behind Hercules' back. "As for the people, I have no idea what is going on."

"Do you think they're servants to the beasts? If so, maybe we should vanquish them as well."

"That would seem to be the obvious answer."

"Good." Hercules flexed his chest. "These pebbles are becoming annoying."

Bracing himself, he prepared to strike at the force.

Just as he did so, a clash of thunder filled the area around him. All of his attackers screamed, almost in unison, and it seemed as if one or two of them passed out. Suddenly standing beside Hercules was a clean-shaven man with a thick mane of gray hair, wearing a bathrobe.

"Dad!" Hercules cried in joy. "You're just in time to help us vanquish these slaves! Hey," Hercules frowned as he studied his father's face, "when did you shave?"

"Hercules!" Zeus nearly exploded with rage at the sight of his son. "Where have you been?"

"What?" Hercules shrugged. "I've just been hanging out with—"

"What are you doing?" Zeus interrupted him, staring at the horrified officers, most of whom huddled on the ground in fear.

Hercules began to become defensive. "I was freeing people from —" he began.

"Do you realize what you have done?" Zeus roared at him once more. "This was a gentle balance, but we've been able to maintain it up and until now! You may have ruined everything!"

"Dad." Hercules tried to look into his father's eyes. "What's going on?"

One of the benefits of having an alternate dimension all to themselves was that there were no more humans trying to reach them. The humans no longer believed in them. To most, the Olympians were only myths and bedtime stories for children. Initially, this had offended Zeus, but after a time, he had come to accept it. Eventually, he had realized it was likely better for both parties. If the humans didn't believe the gods were real, the gods could do what they needed to without the humans getting in the way. No more explanation was needed for great cosmological displays of power, since that was all explained by science now. Great signs and wonders simply ceased to be. When people stopped needing divine explanations for everything, deciding instead there was a scientific reason for all of it, they stopped needing deities. Zeus was all right with that. Science was not really a rival, after all; it was a conduit. He could use science to achieve his goals.

This incident with Hercules, however, threatened everything. They would start looking again. Plus, with scientific technology at the state it was now, they might actually find the pocket dimension.

That would not be pleasant.

"Not now." Zeus glared at Hercules. "We have to get back to Olympus. Come on."

"But Dad," Hercules resisted. "I have to defend the—"

With the same clap of thunder, both Zeus and Hercules vanished.

The police officers pulled themselves off of the ground slowly, carefully examining the frightful scene. Where there had, just moments before, been two crazed madmen, the destroyers of six automobiles with their bare fists, there now remained only one man. This man looked saner than any of the officers felt at the moment.

"Γεια σας." The man waved to them timidly.

A few of the other officers waved back, confused.

"Erm..." The man began to look around, nervously. "Πω πω, ότι ο τύπος ήταν τρελός, έτσι?"[4]

The man chuckled nervously, and a few of the officers joined him, having no idea what this bastard was saying. One of the officers began to raise his pistol again, but another officer stayed his hand. They were not going to fire on an unarmed civilian, especially not one so fascinating.

The thunder filled the area again, and the angry old man from earlier reappeared.

"Έλα Jason,"[5] he growled angrily, taking hold of the man.

"Σας ευχαριστώ!"[6] the man cried, seeming extremely grateful to have not been forgotten.

Both men vanished.

The police force stared at the now-empty scene in disbelief.

"Um, I think that guy," one of the officers stammered, "just said thank you... in Greek?"

"No," the officer next him denied it. "That guy was too... he was too drunk to be speaking Greek."

"Right," said another one. "And on steroids... steroids make you act like that, right?"

"They do," said a fourth. "And, guys, we have to start cracking down on the drug that makes you disappear in a flash, cuz, I mean, that's dangerous, right?"

None of the officers ever forgot what they saw that day.

They don't like to talk about it much.

The news, of course, did not feel the same way.

IV

Hercules was always Zeus' favorite son. That may have been one of the reasons that Hera hated him so much.

Before Hercules was born, Zeus made the proclamation that the next one of his children to be born would one day rule Olympus. Hera noticed that Alcmene was about to give birth with Hercules, so she had to intervene. She went to Lucina, the goddess of childbirth, and told her to hold Alcmene's labor until she could think of something more permanent. Lucina was reluctant at first, but she agreed to do this for Hera.

For a week, Alcmene remained in labor, trying to birth Hercules. Unbeknownst to her, Lucina had placed her otherworldly hands over Alcmene's womb, preventing the child's emergence. During this time, Alcmene screamed in pain, cursing the heavens. Hera looked upon the scene with satisfaction, seeing that Alcmene was very close to death. She deduced that, should Alcmene die, the child in her womb would die as well.

Galanthis, Alcmene's handmaiden, stood by her mistress throughout this entire ordeal. Upon seeing her in such pain, Galanthis sought out the cause. Finding that Lucina was holding her mistress's womb closed, she began to search for ways to loose the bond.

Her opportunity came a few hours later. Lucina had become

tired, being forced to hold the child back for so long. She began to fall to sleep, and as she did, Galanthis cried out in glee.

"Look!" she cheered. "The woman has given birth!"

This startled Lucina so much that she jerked back to awareness, accidentally loosening her hold upon Alcmene's womb for a moment.

In that moment, Hercules was born.

When she found out about the deception, Hera turned Galanthis into a weasel.

That may have been a little over-the-top, but the point was made: You shouldn't make Hera angry.

V

Zeus was not happy.

One would imagine that, after searching for him for the better part of three centuries, a father would be elated to see his son once more. Given the circumstances, however, one can understand his dismay. His world was burning down. Everything was happening so quickly he did not even have time to think. After so long of relatively low activity, having so much of it thrust at him all at once was nerve-racking. He had no idea what Hercules had been doing over the centuries, but at the moment, it did not matter.

As soon as the three of them had successfully navigated the nexus back to Olympus, Zeus turned to his son. Hercules was bent over, coughing from the unexpected shock of being dragged through a portal. For a moment, Zeus' anger was stilled as he moved to where his son was hunched over, and patted him on the back.

"You'll be all right son," Zeus said. "Instant portals are harder to handle than gradual nexuses. You'll get used to it."

"Kind of like I had to get used to beer," Jason suggested. "After a while, I'm sure that you'll actually prefer it."

"Oh, I hate beer." Zeus crinkled his nose as he looked at Jason. "Wine is so much better for you!"

"I agree," Jason replied. "But beer is less expensive, and easier to drink, you know?"

Zeus nodded. "I suppose," he answered. "Still, the benefits of wine are... wait..."

Zeus removed his hand from Hercules' shoulder, and darkness crept across his face. "Where have you two been for the past—" he roared, stopping himself short and shaking his head in anger. "We have to get back to Olympus. I'm sure my wife, your reluctant step-mother, is going to want to hear this."

Hercules straightened himself up slowly. "Hera. How angry is she?"

Zeus' darkening scowl was all the answer Hercules needed.

"Come on!" Zeus commanded, seizing Hercules on the shoulder and dragging him along.

Mount Olympus had not changed all that much. It still had the towering columns, holding up the sky in regal form, and the marble walkways that paved the way through it. As Jason followed Zeus and Hercules, he was amazed by the elegance around him. He had never come to the gods' residence before, and the view was breathtaking. Beautiful statues, carved out of stone, dotted the landscape. There stood in one place a tribute to the titan Atlas with the world atop his shoulders. Elsewhere, the goddess Aphrodite stood with a pale reflection of all of her beauty etched into alabaster.

Exotic plants, no doubt gifts from the goddess Demeter, appeared here and there. Jason was not sure of the origin for most of them, but they were beautiful. One stood roughly five feet from the base of the pot that held it. It was covered in beautiful leaves and flowers, reaching its apex in the form of a macabre mouth. Jason watched in awed horror as the mouth opened and devoured an insect that had dared to fly too closely. What world was this, where even the plants now had their defenses? Jason began to regret coming back from Oblivion or, more appropriately, ever going to Oblivion in the first place.

More sights welcomed him. As they walked, Jason looked to his right and saw some of the Olympus residents lounging on oddly shaped furniture, wearing clothing that was similar to what he had seen on the humans they had encountered when first emerging from the nexus. Up the pathway a bit, the god Eros (or Cupid, as he had begun calling himself) was walking toward them with a cylindrical leaf that appeared to be fire hanging out of his mouth and speaking into one of the shells Jason had seen the humans in the world using. As they passed, Cupid stopped frozen and stared at them with an open jaw. Jason smiled at him sheepishly.

He felt as if he were a foreigner, rather than an exalted hero.

What had become of his world?

Hercules didn't notice these things. He was too distracted by the memory of what befell individuals had angered his dad.

Cupid had been smoking since the Earth year of 3 AD. That was when he and Apollo had gone over to the yet-undiscovered land of what is now known to be South America. Apollo had claimed that there were some warring tribes that needed to be pacified or some such nonsense, but Cupid now suspected that Apollo had just wanted to branch out and see the world beyond the borders of Rome and Greece. Cupid had needed a distraction.

While he was there, Cupid observed smoking through the rituals of the native shamans. They would take the rolled up tobacco leaf, light it on fire, and smoke it. Fascinated, Cupid was loath to experiment at first, but after watching for long enough, he couldn't resist. He inhaled. The smell was horrid and the taste was not anything that one would necessarily desire to have in one's mouth. The rising smoke that filled his nostrils made him nauseous and he began to gag, his eyes filling with tears. It was disgusting.

Cupid took another puff. Yes, it was still disgusting.

Cigars had certainly evolved over the centuries. There were better ways to refine tobacco, better humidors for aging and preserving the texture, flavors and botanicals enhancing the natural ecstasy, and different techniques for wrapping and packing the tobacco that made each cigar distinct. South America still made the best cigars. Nicaragua was Cupid's favorite location. Cubans were all right, but when one was not hindered by the legal and social stipulation that some mortals put on them, they really lost a good bit of their appeal. Nicaraguan cigars were almost certainly his favorite.

Olympus was not a non-smoking atmosphere, mainly because only he and a few others even took part in the activity. Chiron smoked cigarettes, which Cupid had never found appealing. The Oracle of Delphi smoked, but it was not tobacco. Apollo would occasionally join him in a smoke, and hookahs were very popular on the Mount, but Cupid was really the only one who took part in the ritual of cigar smoking regularly. He did not mind smoking alone so much. He just enjoyed his cigars.

Another thing that had never become very popular on the Mount was the cellular phone. A few of the deities had them, and most of them were sponsors or shareholders with their individual carriers. For a time, Cupid had attempted to talk Zeus into carrying their own service, exclusive to the Mount and its residents, but Zeus was still having trouble understanding the advantage of rotary phones, let alone mobile ones. If he wanted to be left alone, he would say, why would he want a buzzing device that connected him to people that he didn't want to talk to anyway? After a while, Cupid had given up.

Cupid casually walked down the marble pathway, toward the gates out of Olympus. He had an Oliva Seria V cigar in his one hand, smoking it slowly, and his cell phone in the other.

"No," he said to the person on the other end, "I don't have any plans tonight. I mean, I might head down to Earth. There's this place in Cleveland that I've been hearing about and I'd like see what the locals are doing, but besides that..."

"*Cupid,*" the chastising voice of Nemesis rang into his ear, "*leave the locals alone. I'm familiar with the place in Cleveland; you should come out with me.*"

Cupid chuckled. Although she would never admit it, Nemesis was always looking for an excuse to cut loose. While a club was not the most rebellious of activities, it still counted in her book. Cupid figured that she would justify the occasion by saying that she was trying to keep him out of trouble. Cupid was convinced that she was really just using that as an excuse to get out and get a little crazy. Ever since her role as Vengeance Avatar had been virtually usurped by mortal enforcements, she had begun to feel a little unappreciated. She was probably making up for that by playing morality police to the gods.

"How do you know I was going to do something filthy?" Cupid laughed. "Maybe the place the locals were talking about was a coffee shop. Did you ever think of that?"

"*First off, I know you were doing something filthy because you're Cupid.*" Nemesis' moral superiority rang through. "*Second, it's downtown Cleveland, and there's only one place that you would go out of your way to appear there. I think that you'd be better off coming out with me.*"

"Why can't you just say that you're lonely, and you want some company?" Cupid teased her. "Not everything has to be an excuse to—"

Cupid stopped short and stared, unashamedly, at what was approaching him. Zeus stormed toward him, with an individual in tow and a second following closely behind him. The two individuals looked disgusting, as if they had not bathed or changed their clothing (or fashion sense) in centuries. His jaw hit the marble walkway as they passed him. The second man saw him watching, and gave him a hesitant smile, followed by a half-wave. Cupid dazedly waved back.

"Cupid," Nemesis' voice prodded him. "*You stopped talking. Is something the matter?*"

Cupid paused for a moment longer, slowly considering what could be happening.

"I'm going to have to call you back," he said, hanging up the phone before he heard the response.

He had always just assumed that both Hercules and Jason had died. Granted, it was likely they would have heard about it if a son of Zeus had died, but with the transition through dimensions, it was possible the news could have gotten lost. It had been two and a half centuries. Even Zeus had given up searching for the most part. Hercules was, at one point, Zeus' favorite son. He had searched for centuries, wandering the human dimension, looking under every stone and twig, only to come back with nothing. No one had any idea where Hercules was.

This being the case, one can imagine Cupid's disbelief at seeing the fallen hero, risen from the grave. Very few had actually accomplished that.

"Hey," Cupid signaled to Morpheus, the god of dreams, who was standing across the courtyard, "was that who I think it was?"

Morpheus' shaggy, silver-maned head turned to Cupid with a frown. He had been considering if, one day, he would be able to transmit dreams into a computer's sleep mode. It did not seem likely, since artificial intelligence would likely have artificial dreams. Upon further consideration of the process, Morpheus had determined a computer's stages of sleep. First stage would likely be the screen saver, where a simple keystroke or twitch of the mouse would rouse it once more. A computer's sleep mode resembled the fourth stage, or deep sleep. Waking it from this took a bit more effort. If a computer had an REM function, it would occur during this stage. If Morpheus were ever able to implant dreams into a computer's "mind" (functional hard drive), it would be most plausible during this stage. He had been considering a technique to do just that when Cupid interrupted his thought process.

"What are you talking about, Cupid?" Morpheus asked, annoyed at being disturbed. "Was who what?"

"That guy." Cupid pointed in the direction that Zeus and his captives had disappeared. "He looked just like Hercules... and the guy behind him looked like Jason! The guy with the Fleece, remember?"

"Of course I remember." Morpheus nodded, walking toward Cupid, and reluctantly gazing in the direction that Cupid indicated. "I also remember they're dead. They've been dead for centuries."

"That was never proven," Cupid insisted, continuing to stare after Zeus. "We just assumed."

"I would have thought two millennia would be proof enough." Morpheus sighed. "Also, Jason is still human; he was never granted immortality. There's no way that he could have survived this long, especially not in a mobile and recognizable state."

Cupid rolled his eyes. "You know," he said, "for being the god of dreams, you don't really have much of an imagination."

"When you live in a world of dreams," Morpheus answered the rebuke, looking down at Cupid from the four or five inches that he stood over him with a sly grin, "you find reality anywhere that you can."

"Go to hell," Cupid sneered.

"There is no hell," Morpheus said, condescendingly. "Only Tartarus."

"Whatever." Cupid turned away, giving up the argument. "It's just an expression. I know what I saw, and I saw Hercules."

"You're dreaming," Morpheus teased.

As Cupid walked away, he saluted Morpheus, using another fairly modern technique, which required only one finger. Morpheus shook his head and stared in the direction that Cupid had been looking. Perhaps he was being too unimaginative. Still, it was impossible to think that, after so long, Hercules and Jason had returned. It simply did not make sense.

VI

The great hall of Olympus, where the gods would sit and hold their council, had not changed all that much. There were still twelve thrones positioned in a semi-circle, one for each of the Olympians. It was rare now, however, that any of them were occupied, save for

46

Zeus' and Hera's, which sat side-by-side, a bit higher than the rest. Some scholars had speculated that Eros (or Cupid) might have been included in this circle, alongside his mother, Aphrodite, but this assessment was inaccurate. Cupid had never wanted the responsibility of being included with the Olympians. Since the gods' departure from the Earthly plane, Aphrodite's seat had remained vacant.

Hera sat on her throne in the great hall, alone. In spite of herself, she wore a little smile upon her thin lips. Seeing Hercules create so much chaos in the world had made her feel practically giddy. Yes, it threatened everything that they had established over the centuries, but that was beside the point. It had provided entertainment, it had proven Hercules' incompetence, and it had inadvertently made Zeus look like an ass. There was almost no downside.

For the moment, Hera was alone. Zeus would be back with his son soon, and he would not be happy. Hera wanted to witness the scene.

The door to the great hall shuddered as it slammed open with a loud bang. Zeus stormed in with a protesting Hercules in tow. Jason followed a few feet behind, looking sheepishly from side-to-side.

"Do you have any idea of the responsibilities that you've abandoned?" Zeus roared at his son as he charged toward his throne. He dropped Hercules off directly in front of his throne, and sat down next to Hera, whose smile widened slightly. Possibly, this was because of Hercules getting yelled at, or perhaps it was the sight of Jason. She'd always been particularly fond of him. Hera could not decide which pleased her more!

"Dad," Hercules defended himself. "I do not see what the problem is here. I was gone for a little while, sure, and maybe a little longer than I should have been. Come on, though, I came back, and look: I just saved six humans from these monsters!"

"They're called cars," Zeus informed him, feeling his face growing red.

"Fine." Hercules threw up his confused hands. "I just saved six humans from these cars! I don't see what the—"

"They're not monsters!" Zeus roared. "They're vehicles!"

The pride of his victory drained from Hercules' face as reality found a place in his head. Had he charged in half-cocked? Perhaps he should have analyzed the situation a bit more before he had simply attacked the things that he had assumed to be beasts. He was a hero, was he not? It was his duty to save the oppressed. The people had appeared to be oppressed! It was a logical step to think that these monsters/cars were the creatures doing the oppression. Still, considering the alien world which they had stepped into, perhaps he should have taken a moment to calculate the situation.

"Oh," was the final summation of his thoughts as his eyes fell from his father's angry glare. "There is no way that I could have known that," he continued, attempting to return his eyes to their former location.

"That does explain the reaction, though," Jason said from where he stood beside Hercules.

"Hello, Jason," Hera greeted the hero. Her smile widened a bit more. "How are you?"

"Oh, hello, Hera." Jason flashed his shining white smile at her. "My, you look well. Have you discovered the fountain of youth?"

Jason winked at her flirtatiously, and Hera giggled girlishly.

"Yes I have," she answered. "It's called *Clinique*."

"Hey." Hercules swatted the back of Jason's head. "Stop flirting with my stepmom!"

"I'm not!" Jason defended himself, recovering from the undeserved blow. "I was giving her a compliment! Hercules, you know that I am a happily married man!"

At the mention of marriage, Jason's mind went quickly to his wife Medea. Given how much the world had changed, would she still be alive? Would she still be his? In order for the world to have changed so much, they must have been gone for a long time, much longer than anticipated. How old was she now? Would she even recognize him? Jason assumed that he would be sleeping on the cot for at least a month.

Still, he longed to see her once more.

"Silence!" Zeus' voice thundered through the room, directing all attention to himself once more.

"I am going to ask you a series of questions," Zeus continued, lowering a chilling and frustrated scowl upon his son. "I want you to answer them as directly and as simply as possible. You will not speak between questions, you will answer only the questions that I ask, and you will ask no questions of your own. Are we understood?"

"Yes, sir." Hercules fought to sound humble. His foul must have been larger than he had at first assumed.

Jason fell to silence by his side, feeling anxious.

Zeus posed his first question: "Where have you been?"

"The Oblivion Tavern, sir."

Out of the corner of his eye, Jason caught a glimpse of Hera. The satisfied smile that had graced her lips when they had first entered disappeared, replaced by a wrathful fire that nearly burned from within her eyes. In that instant, Jason realized one thing: they had done something incredibly wrong.

"What were you doing at the tavern?"

Jason did not feel as if this question truly needed to be asked, but he wisely kept his mouth shut.

"We were drinking... sir?"

"Do you have any idea how long you have been there?"

Hercules chose his answer carefully. It was fairly obvious to him now that they had been gone longer than he had expected to be gone. He selected an answer that he thought to be exaggerated.

"One year, sir."

If possible, Zeus' scowl darkened. He repeated the question: "Any idea how long you have been there?"

Breathing deep, Hercules chose an answer that seemed more impossible. "A decade, sir."

Zeus leaned forward in his throne. "Any idea?" he roared.

Hercules began to grow afraid. He began to tremble despite himself. He had never seen his father this angry, especially not at him. Still, a response had been demanded. Hercules answered as he likely should have answered at the start.

"Too long, sir."

"Two thousand years!" Zeus answered his own question.

Jason physically felt the blood in his veins drop down to his feet as he became pale as a sheet, and his life began to flash before his eyes. "Two thousand..." he stammered. "Where is my wife?"

"Medea was human, Jason," Hera answered, the adoration which she had felt before now gone from her voice. "After two thousand years, where do you expect that she is?"

"No!" Jason cried in agony. "That cannot be! This is a game, is it not? This is one of those games that you play with mortals sometimes! You arranged for Morpheus to provide a waking dream, so that we could be taught a lesson. Once we leave, we will find the world as we left it." Jason laughed desperately. "It was a good joke, father Zeus." He shuddered, not believing it himself. "Consider the lesson learned. Yes, ha ha, a good joke indeed. Now, where is Medea?"

"Ask any of the Olympians," Zeus answered, turning his stare to Jason. "They will take you to where she rests."

Jason raced from the great hall without another word.

"It is nice to see one so concerned for his neglected wife," Hera remarked, after watching Jason's dramatic exit.

"Two thousand years?" Hercules exclaimed in shock. "That is... that is longer than the rule of Greece! How could we have been gone for so long? Why did you not come to get me?"

Zeus shook his head. "I looked for you everywhere, son," he said, sorrowfully. "I could find you nowhere."

"Did you search for me at Oblivion?"

"Of course I searched for you at..." Zeus paused in his rebuke. He did not care for Oblivion much, mainly because no one cared to have him there. He was a famous killjoy, and many of those who frequented Oblivion avoided him. It was possible he had neglected Oblivion in his search.

"Did you see how Jason ran off to find his wife?" Hera interrupted Zeus. "He is certainly devoted to his relationship and willing to take responsibility for what he has done. It's nice to see a man who cares so much for his marital responsibilities."

"Yes." Hercules turned to Hera, frowning sarcastically. "It's nice to see how quickly he abandoned me, when we were both responsible for this. It is good to have a brother who cares so much for—"

"Wait," he slowly picked up what Hera was inferring. "Where is my wife? Where is Hebe?"

Before Hera could answer, Zeus rose from his throne and advanced to where Hercules was standing. "That is not your concern right now," he said. "You, Hercules, have abandoned your responsibilities. You have left this world for centuries to pursue your own self-ish, hedonistic desires. You told no one where you were going, and you thought nothing of those who would be concerned by your absence. I scoured the globe, asking all that could be found of news of you, and no information could be provided. The world has moved on countless times since you've been gone, and yet here you stand, as if nothing has happened."

Reaching out for his prodigal son, Zeus pulled Hercules into his arms.

"Welcome home, son," he said as he embraced Hercules, holding him tightly against his chest.

"Thanks, Dad," Hercules said, as he returned the embrace.

"What?" Hera screeched as she flew from her throne. "His absence could be the reason we're in the state we're in right now! If he had been present during the war of the gods, the result may have been swayed in our favor! You know that! Where is your wrath, husband? There must be retribution!"

Ending the hug, Zeus turned to his angry wife. "He is my son, Hera," he replied firmly. "Be assured that consequences will come in their time. For now, allow me to simply be glad that he has returned."

"Thank you, Father." Hercules smiled from ear to ear. Some-where, in the back of his head, he had heard Hera say something about a war he could have helped with, but he paid very little attention to it.

"Wait..." Hercules considered what he had just heard. "Consequences?"

Hera sighed with exasperation. "You make me sick," she growled at Zeus as she collapsed back into her throne.

"I know," Zeus affirmed.

"So, Dad." Hercules tapped Zeus' shoulder nervously. "It's great to be back, let me tell you. My, how I have missed this place! Did you say something about consequences?"

"They will come in time, be sure of it," Zeus said, turning back to Hercules. "For now, just be glad to be home. I have to spend some time with my wife now. Why do you not go and explore the mountain? Much has changed while you have been away. I'm sure that your friends will be happy to see you."

Hercules opened his mouth as if to pursue the subject, but the look in his father's eyes convinced him this would be a bad idea. He turned to leave the hall.

"Hercules," Hera called as he was about to exit.

He turned to her reluctantly.

"Stay out of the wine closet," she sneered. "People have been known to get lost in there."

Without a word, Hercules turned and walked out of the throne room.

After he was gone, Zeus turned to his wife. "That was not necessary," he informed her.

"Oh, I know." Hera smirked. "It was still fun. Besides, he earned it. I know you're just going to let him off with a stern scolding, if that. It's likely the consequence I have to look forward to."

"I allowed him to go through twelve labors for something that was less than thirty-percent his fault," Zeus replied coldly. "Do you really think I'm going to let him off easy?"

"Yes," Hera said, turning her cold glare on her husband. "That's your pattern, isn't it? Besides that, this changes our plans completely, doesn't it? There's no way we could go through with it now."

"I don't see why not." Zeus shrugged. "I mean, he never factored into the plans before. Why should this alter our lives?"

"He's your favorite son!"

"Maybe it's time to cut the leash. After all, has he not proven that he can survive in the world by himself? Maybe I'll just send him back to Oblivion."

Hera smiled wickedly. "Oh," she said, "that's cold."

Zeus interlocked his fingers and cracked his knuckles. "I have my times," he said, smiling slyly.

Most of the time, Hera could not stand her husband. He could be such an idiot! There were times, however, when she remembered why she loved him.

VII

A long, long time ago...

Zeus took another step up the hill. It was a long and tedious trek, but it was one he felt necessary. Generally, he did not like consulting the Oracle of Delphi, mostly because she spoke in riddles, very rarely telling him anything. Right now, though, he was out of options.

The day was not a bad day. The sky was blue, birds were singing, and the ground beneath his feet was clothed in green foliage, welcoming his every footstep. The Oracle had made it a point to have her patio built atop a particularly steep hill. To this end, no one could reach her but those who were dedicated to their journey. If she had made the location more accessible, she never would have been left alone. Everyone would have come to her to seek their future, and she would have had no time to herself. This way, only those who truly desired her guidance would come. The hill was particularly steep, and Zeus did not enjoy making the effort. As the leader of the gods, he should not have to. He should be able to simply will himself to the location he desired, and * POOF * he would appear there. However, the Oracle had been very precise about such efforts, especially in regards to gods and such doing exactly that. Zeus believed she mostly wanted to be left alone.

Coming to the apex of the mountain, where the Oracle's plateau was situated, Zeus laid the laurel branch by the entrance. This was her usual accepted payment. It had to be a true laurel branch as well, so Zeus could not simply take an oak branch and convert it to laurel, as he likely would have done. It was not that the laurel tree was so difficult to find, it was just so much easier to use something close at hand. To find a laurel branch, one first had to locate a laurel tree. When you're a god, it's much easier to simply use what's at hand. That was probably why the Oracle demanded a true laurel branch. There seemed to be a lot of stipulations regarding this consultation, and it hardly seemed worth the effort. Still, this is what was ordered.

Zeus could see the Oracle from where he stood. She was as beautiful as ever, with her soft brown hair tossing in the wind, and her white gown wrapped tightly around her flawless figure. She was kneeling at an altar, built above a chasm in the ground, from which spewed the steams providing her insights. Zeus could see her breathing deeply as he approached. She knew he was there. There was a good chance she had known even before he had made the decision to come. Still, she did not a acknowledge him. It was all part of the game.

When he was within a few feet from her, Zeus chose to break the silence. "Hello, Pythia," he greeted her.

The Oracle raised her head from the mists and smiled her lackadaisical smile, revealing a small dimple on each cheek. The Oracle never seemed to age. Perhaps it was the mists that kept her so young and beautiful. Upon seeing Zeus, she rose gracefully to her feet and approached him.

"Zeus," she greeted him in her musical voice. "Leader of the gods. You honor both myself and Delphi by coming again so soon."

54

The riddles had begun already. Zeus frowned at The Oracle. "I have not been here in decades."

"Oh." The Oracle's smile faltered for a moment, but then returned in full force. "Perhaps that is true. I have not been paying much attention."

Pythia continued to approach Zeus until she was close enough to embrace him, kissing him gently through the beard on his cheek. After this show of affection, she turned and began to walk back to her altar.

"It is hard to keep track when time is so non-sequential," she continued her explanation. "Or perhaps we are simply not meant to be chronological."

Zeus followed her toward the altar, watching as she knelt over the chasm once more and inhaled. After the inhalation, she returned her attention to him.

"I assume that there is a reason for your journey?" she prodded him. "Very few make the passage to simply be in my company."

"I cannot imagine they do." Zeus looked back at the hill with a sigh. "It seems like you've taken great efforts to discourage people from doing exactly that."

"I do like my time to not be wasted," the Oracle said, smiling. "And, to that end..."

"Ah, yes." Zeus proceeded to approach the altar. He had always wondered about the mists. If he were to inhale them, would he see the future as well?

"I have scoured the Earth," he continued with his reason for coming. "I have searched everywhere for my son—"

"Hercules," the Oracle interrupted, revealing the son's identity.

"Yes, Hercules," Zeus confirmed. "There is no corner in which I have not searched. Still, my son remains lost."

"Hercules is not lost," the Oracle informed Zeus, diverting herself to the mists once more and breathing in deeply. "You assume that, simply because you are unable to locate him, he is lost. He is not. Hercules knows exactly where he is."

"Oh!" Zeus raised his eyebrows in surprise. He had all but

assumed his son was dead. It seemed the only logical option, since there was no evidence of him anywhere to be found on Earth. "Do you know where he is?"

As soon as the words were out of his mouth, Zeus regretted saying them.

The Oracle looked up from her fumes with a cynical and insultingly furrowed brow.

Zeus dropped his gaze. "I did not need to ask you that," he muttered, "did I?"

"Did you need to ask The Oracle of Delphi whether she knew about that of which you came to inquire?" The Oracle turned her offended head back to the mists. "No, you did not need to ask that. If I wish to know something, that something is what I know. You are aware of this. It does not matter, though; you have your answer."

"I have nothing," Zeus disagreed with her, beginning to become frustrated. "I need to know where my son is! You have just told me you know!"

The Oracle nodded. "I do."

"Then tell me," Zeus insisted.

The Oracle shook her head. "I already have," she insisted, looking at Zeus once more. "Your son is not lost, nor is he hiding. He simply does not wish to be disturbed. He is not doing anything that you would call important, yet he wishes to continue doing it for a time. That is all I will tell you for now."

"You have told me nothing." Zeus did his best to remain calm. It did very little good to become angry with the Oracle.

"You have asked me for the location of your son," The Oracle reiterated, inhaling the fumes once more. "I provided you with the state of his mind. His mind is located at a very safe place right now. If you had wanted his physical location, perhaps you ought to have been more specific in your question."

"I need his physical location to be here."

"You will always have desires," the Oracle said with a laugh.

"Some things are simply more important than those. Your son is safe, I can assure you of that."

Zeus sighed again, turning from the altar. "Hera told me that this would be a waste of time," he grumbled, taking a step toward the hill, preparing to make the descent.

"The assurance of your son's safety does not make this visit worthwhile?" the Oracle asked.

Zeus paused and turned back to look into her stunning eyes once more. One had an iris of gold, revealing the past, and the other of silver, a reflection of the future. Peering into them, Zeus wished he could see the answers locked within. They remained a mystery, only eyes.

"I was simply hoping for something more," he concluded his session, turning around again and continuing his passage down the hill. The knowledge of Hercules' safety did comfort him a bit, but not as much as it should have.

To be honest, although he was pleased that Hercules was safe, it hardly seemed to matter. He only knew that Hercules was not there. He wanted his son back.

Good evening, ladies and gentlemen, I'm James Novus. Tonight, we have an update on the "Gladiator" incident from a couple days ago. For those of you who missed it, the story involved a slew of destroyed cars, members of the 5th precinct police force, and a couple of oddly dressed men, apparently playing Gladiator, with the automobiles as their lions. The two spoke in an unidentifiable language and our reporter on scene, Candace Amentia, had translated this as drunken or drugged blathering. Now, it seems that diagnosis may have been a bit hasty. I'm here with local college professor, Dr.

Robert Sanus, who has a different interpretation of the events. What do you make of it, doctor?

Thank you for having me on your show this evening, James. After studying the video, I feel confident in saying that the gladiators, as you call them, are not speaking gibberish. In fact, they seem to be communicating with each other in a form of ancient Greek. As you can see here, the larger of the two is asking his partner why the police are attacking them. If you can go back a bit... right there! Yes, the smaller man seems to be expecting praise from the drivers, as if he had done them a favor in destroying their vehicles. Unfortunately, the driver probably did not have "Destroyed by crazed warriors" in their insurance policies (ha ha). On more than one occasion during the combat, the larger of the two referred to the other as "Jason," while Jason called him "Hercules," perhaps referring to the son of Zeus. It seems obvious to me that these two are—

Thank you, Dr. Sanus, for your astute analysis. Unfortunately, we have to go to a commercial break. When we return, a large drug company claims to have cured obesity. Their new pill not only destroys the fat, it prevents the accumulation of any extra fat at all without diet or exercise. Find out how to get lean with no more effort, while sitting in front of your television. We'll return with the secret in a moment.

CHAPTER THREE

I

MEDEA WAS THE DAUGHTER OF KING AEETES, RULER OF THE island kingdom of Colchis. Her story really begins when Jason, along with the Argonauts, came to Colchis.

Upon the island of Colchis was a sacred item: The Golden Fleece. The Fleece had been worn by a winged ram. It was said that this ram had rescued Phrixus and Helle, the two children of King Athamas of Halos, from their tyrannical stepmother and flown them to safety on the island. After this event, the ram, who was created by Poseidon, the great god of the sea, was shaved. His fleece was then placed in a grove, and a dragon was stationed outside of the grove to protect it. In all of the kingdom, there was nothing that King Aeetes treasured more than this Fleece.

After Jason had presented himself to the reigning king of Iolkos, along with announcing that he desired his father's kingdom, Pelias had demanded that, should Jason be sincere, he retrieve the Golden Fleece from Colchis. Pelias may have believed that the mission was too impossible, Jason would not be able to complete it, or he may have simply wanted the treasure for himself. Whatever Pelias' motive, Jason had his quest. He set off upon it with no doubt he would complete it fully.

Upon arriving at Colchis, Jason approached King Aeetes with his request to retrieve the Fleece, and present it to King Pelias. Medea was present in the throne room during this meeting, and the sight of such a handsome man left her speechless. As he addressed her father, Medea felt herself filled with desire for the brave rogue.

King Aeetes felt insulted by Jason's very presence, let alone his request to remove such a valued treasure. In mockery, he made three impossible demands: First, he had to sow a field with fire-breathing oxen (which he had to yoke by himself). Second, he had to plant the teeth of a dragon into the freshly sown field (which would not seem so bad, except that the teeth grew into an entire army, which Jason then had to figure out how to defeat). Finally, he had to get past the dragon, which never slept, that guarded the Fleece. Medea's heart sank when she saw the look upon Jason's downcast face. As her father sat back on his throne, satisfied that the Fleece would remain in his possession, Jason left the throne room. As he walked out, Medea felt as if her heart were leaving with him.

That night, after her father had fallen to sleep, Medea crept to the Argonauts' camp. There, she saw them preparing, but not to leave, as Medea had first suspected. They were attempting to formulate an idea on how to yoke the oxen without becoming fried. Medea approached Jason directly. Jason recognized her immediately as the king's daughter. He was about to throw her from the camp so she could not hear their plans, thus betraying them to her father. Before he could do that, however, Medea presented her offer: she would provide ways to complete each of the quests if, in return, she was permitted to leave Colchis on *The Argos* once they were completed.

Jason agreed to her offer. After all, who would refuse such a beautiful young lady?

II

The night was cold. In the sky, a thin layer of clouds accented the full moon. A light sprinkle fell to the ground, dampening the soft grass beneath Jason's feet. A cool breeze blew through the air, ruffling his filthy and disheveled hair.

Jason felt nothing.

After leaving the throne room, he had approached Artemis, the huntress and goddess of the moon. She had regarded at him with pity-filled eyes and a sorrowful frown. At first, she would not answer him, but Jason pressed her for an answer, becoming more and more concerned as he continued. Finally, Artemis gave him the location.

Now, he stood at that place, looking with a mixture of sorrow, shame, loss, and utter loneliness at his wife's headstone.

Here Lies Medea
Forsaken love will not be forgotten again
May she Rest in Peace

After revealing Medea's final resting place, Artemis had told Jason the story of her demise. Medea had not given up hope her husband would return to her until she was on her deathbed, at the age of forty-two, more than ten years after Jason had left her. Only then did she finally abandoned her dream of a joyful reunion. As she lay there, with the disease now known to be breast cancer ravaging her body, she cursed him and the day she had met him. It broke Jason's heart to learn that Medea thought he had abandoned her. It broke his heart even more to think she was technically right. As he stood in the soft rain in the cold graveyard, staring at the frozen headstone, another type of moisture began to cover his face. He had destroyed that which was most important to him, his companion, and now he was alone. There was nothing he could do. He continued to stand, tears streaming from his reddened eyes. There was nowhere else for him to be.

"I'm sorry," he sobbed, as if the words would somehow mean something. "I never left you. I love you, Medea. I'm sorry."

Choking on tears and rain, Jason sat down upon the gravestone.

An unearthly chill crept through the air, filling the graveyard. It was not the wind, nor a drop in temperature. Those who could feel it would say that the chill came from inside of them, as if their body were fighting the urge to simply give up and stop working. A new figure, hardly a stranger to the graveyard, had entered. The girl stood a mere four feet from the ground, with golden curls bouncing from her head and silver sparkling eyes. She was dressed in a wide blue and white dress, as if on her way to church on a Sunday morning, or a tea party with her friends. Her skin was pale, as was her frozen smile. As Jason saw the figure approaching, his heart was filled with rage. This was Thanatos, the specter of death.

"She cannot hear you, Jason," the musically childish voice told him. "She's gone now."

Thanatos stopped in her advance to pick up a flower from a grave. With a smile, she gazed at it as the flower began to drain of life. When it was fully dead, Thanatos set the stem back where she had first gotten it.

"I like flowers," she said, returning her gaze to Jason. "But they do not seem to like me so much. Do you know why that is?"

"Why did you do it, Thanatos?" Jason roared angrily, as he jumped from the headstone.

"I told you." Thanatos shrugged. "I like flowers."

"Why did you take her?" Jason continued his rage, oblivious to Thanatos' comment. "She did not have to go that way, as if she were abandoned. She deserved better!"

"I agree." Thanatos nodded. "Medea was a beautiful person, and I took no pleasure in taking her. However, her body was tired of living, and thus, she required my services."

Jason stood over the little girl, as menacingly as possible. "You could have refused her," he growled.

Thanatos giggled impishly, clearly unmoved by the display of testosterone. "I could have, yes," she said, "but I chose not to. I often choose not to, as the occupants of this graveyard would tell you, had they still lips to speak."

Jason turned away, frustrated with his inability to intimidate. "You could have made an exception," he continued, irrationally. "She was your friend."

The guise of the innocent girl faded slightly as her sweet silver eyes melted away, replaced by ink-black orbs. Jason turned back to face Thanatos, and the chill returned to rattle his bones.

"You are my friend, Jason," the figure informed him, voice drained of glee. "I only call you this because you do not fear me as others do. Do not confuse my relationship with you as a bond with your wife. I do not honor marriage, nor any earthly union. Medea meant nothing to me.

"You are my friend, it is true, but even you will one day have need of me, and I shall not refuse you either. On that day, you will walk with me, and your body will decay, turning to dust, as bodies do. You will die, and perhaps then, you will be reunited with your forsaken bride."

In a sudden flood of emotion, Jason fell to his knees before Thanatos. "Take me now," he demanded, offering himself to her.

The silver returned to her eyes as Thanatos playfully raised her index finger to his face. If Jason felt fear, it was eclipsed by his desire to see his Medea once more. This was not how he had expected to die, but it was the only way now. This alien world was not his own, and he wanted nothing to do with it. As he felt Death's finger tracing his face, his body pulsed viciously, resisting the pull. Jason closed his eyes, wanting Death's release.

Thanatos' finger pressed itself into his nose, and she emitted a "BOOP" sound. At the sound, the chills vanished. Jason opened his surprised eyes to see Thanatos' broadly smiling face, shaking her head at him.

"No," she said. "Your mouth desires me, but your mind does not.

There is still much for you to do here. You do not truly want me, you tease."

Tossing her head with playful indignation, Thanatos turned and began to walk away.

Jason reached out for her. "There is nothing left for me here!" he cried out, desperately.

"Perhaps there is." Thanatos looked back at him without stopping her exit. "Perhaps there is not. It changes nothing, teaser. Goodbye."

Thanatos abandoned the distraught hero kneeling in the fresh mud, covered in tears and rain. Jason watched her leave, unsure of how to proceed. Getting to his feet, he turned to Medea's grave once more. He stretched himself out before the headstone, separated from his bride by six feet of dirt. There he lay, crying into the ground, as if his tears could somehow revive his love.

III

Hercules stepped from the bathing chamber, feeling great and smelling much better than he had when he entered. The modern accommodations had not been difficult to translate. Soap was still soap, after all. The cloth to rub it on, dispensing it then onto one's body, was a logical additive. Shampoo was new, at least in the format that it was presented, as was conditioner. Still, these items had held very little challenge, since the instructions were fairly clear as to how to use them: scrub them into one's hair. Hercules performed this ritual twice, enjoying the smells.

Stepping from the shower, Hercules was then met with a challenge: the three-bladed razor. Seeing himself in the mirror had been a shock at first, since he had been used to reflections in more primitive glass fragments, or in pools of water. He was amazed at how handsome he was. Of course, that was a regular occurrence, even in less adequate reflective devices. After the shower, he wrapped a towel about his torso, as his father had shown him how to do, and moved to the water dispensary Zeus had referred to as the sink. The mirror hung above and behind the sink. Hercules gazed at his reflection as he picked up the razor that had been provided. Bringing it to his face, he ran it along his left jawline. To his amazement, the hair that had been there before disappeared. Turning to the razor, he discovered the hair, trapped between the three parallel blades. He had shaved in the old world, of course, but never with such a device as this. It had always been with a single razor blade, and it had hardly been this comfortable.

Hercules proceeded with the shaving ritual, completing it by splashing the after-shave fluid on his face, as his father had shown him. It burned at first, but cooled a moment later. After recovering from the burn, Hercules picked up the tube that contained the white paste. Turning to the brush that lay beside the water dispenser, Hercules smeared the paste on it, just as Zeus had shown him. The paste smelled exotic and tempting. Unable to resist the temptation, Hercules squeezed a small amount of the paste into his mouth. Swishing it around, he found that the taste was not bad either. He swallowed a fair amount of the paste before proceeding with the scrubbing of his teeth, as he had been shown.

The clothing that had been provided for him seemed strange. Hercules could not imagine why someone would want their legs in such restrictive garments. With his tunic, he had much better range of motion, and it made much more sense. He felt imprisoned, wearing these clothes, which his father had called "jeans." Now, the boxers that Zeus had told him to wear underneath the jeans were much more realistic. Perhaps he would just wear them from now on, and forget the jeans completely.

Shoes looked as though they were going to be complicated. Hercules opted to wear the sandals that Zeus had provided as an alternative.

Walking from the room that he had been given to prepare himself in, Hercules was immediately aware of the stares and whispered comments that seemed to follow him. After discovering how long he had been gone, he was not surprised. Zeus said he had been looking for him all over the Earth, which would have been known all around the Mount. As he was walking, he did feel a little bit guilty. He did have responsibilities he had neglected, and that was disappointing. He could not wait to see Hebe again. She at least would be happy to see him. Of course, she was Hera's daughter. Perhaps she would be bothered that he had not told her where he was going? Either way, Hercules was confident that he would be happy to see her.

Zeus and Hera had suggested Medea, Jason's wife, had died. Medea had been mortal, so it was reasonable. Hebe was Hera's daughter, which made her half-god, at very least. Surely, she would not be dead. It was nearly impossible to kill a god, and only half as difficult to kill one of their offspring. Hercules had no idea who Hebe's father was, but given Hera's taste in men, he was likely not just some average human. She was doing fine, wherever she was, he was certain of it. He was certain of it.

Walking through the Mount, he heard a sound he was familiar with. It was music, the beautiful sound of an expertly played instrument (lyre? harp? no, something else...) coming from around the corner, accompanied by a baritone voice. As Hercules recognized the voice, a smile crept across his lips. He stepped a bit quicker as he searched for the voice's owner.

Around the next corner, he spotted the vocalist: Apollo, sitting on a stool, strumming a stringed instrument that he recognized from Oblivion's stage, which was seated on his knee. He believed he remembered Dionysus referring to it as a guitar. Hercules approached Apollo, who looked up at him and smiled. Hercules recognized the song and joined in. As the two of them sang, the air filled with the voices of Muses and instrumentation beyond what they were supplying. When the god of music played a song, the air supplied the music that was absent from the tune.

Are you going to Scarborough fair?
Sing parsley, sage, rosemary, and thyme
Remember me to the one who lives there

For she was once the true love of mine

Hercules followed Apollo's song as best he could, although anything beyond the first verse was a bit foreign to him. They had played it several times at Oblivion, but Hercules had not paid as close of attention to anything beyond verse one.

Tell her to buy me an acre of land
Sing parsley, sage, rosemary, and thyme
Between the salt water and the sea strands
Then she shall be the true love of mine

Apollo looked at him with a snicker as Hercules fumbled over the lyrics. For a verse, he stopped singing and joined in only in harmony, as if to tease Hercules for not knowing the song better. As if complementing their efforts, the faint whispers of Muses echoed the words that Hercules fumbled over.

Tell her to bind it in a sickle of leather (War billows, blazing
*   in scarlet battalions)*
Sing parsley, sage, rosemary, and thyme (Generals order their
*   soldiers to kill)*
And gather it all in a bunch of heather (A soldier cleans and
*   polishes a gun)*
Then she shall be the true love of mine

For the final chorus, they simply repeated the first stanza. Hercules was confident in that, and the two of them sang, joined by the orchestra of the air.

After completing the song, Apollo set his guitar aside, stood up, and embraced his long lost brother. "Hercules!" he exclaimed. "Wow, it's good to see you! It's been centuries! You still cannot sing, though."

Hercules laughed. "Well, coming from the God of Music, I guess that's not much of an insult."

After the embrace, Apollo stepped back to examine his prodigal brother. "Where is your shirt, man?" he asked cynically. "You're really not that good-looking."

"Yes I am," Hercules countered, flexing his right bicep jokingly. "And... well, I could not really figure out how to wear the top garment. I am sure there will be plenty of time to figure it out later."

"I don't know, man," Apollo scoffed, returning to his seat and picking up his guitar again. "Shirts are some of the most complex developments of the modern age. If you can figure out shirts, quantum-physics and astronomical parallax will be a breeze."

Hercules did not understand even half of the words Apollo had just used, but he was growing accustomed to that, so he did not say anything.

"So," Apollo continued, strumming random chord sequences on his guitar, "*Scarborough Fair* is a fairly modern song, relatively speaking. I mean, last time I saw you, the songs from that Jewish King were still pretty popular. How did you learn it?"

"Oblivion," Hercules answered.

"The bar?" Apollo laughed, pausing his strumming to look with disbelief into Hercules' honest eyes. "Is that where you were? Oh my god, that's... that's so wrong! Dad searched the entire globe at least three times, and a million different other places! He couldn't find anything!"

Hercules frowned. "Oblivion is a pretty popular place," he said. "You would have thought he'd have looked there."

"Most of the Olympians don't like Oblivion too much," Apollo reasoned. "Dad went there for a while, but nobody would talk to him. Plus, Mom would give him a hard time whenever he came home, either about hitting on the nymphs or neglecting his duties. Finally, he gave up and stopped going. I don't think I've ever seen Dionysus happier, honestly. Dad's apparently a famous killjoy. I do believe Dad sent an envoy there to look for you, though."

Hercules thought back over his time in Oblivion. He could have sworn that he saw Ares there, and Artemis had come with Orion as well. Maybe the Field of Sobriety had caused them to forget seeing him there, or perhaps they had simply not noticed him. If Zeus had been as concerned as Apollo claimed he was, would he not be something people would have noticed and remembered? The world had changed so much in his absence. Was it his fault?

"What happened to the world, Apollo?" Hercules asked the musician. "I do not even recognize it any longer. It is as if my world were destroyed, and replaced by this new chaos."

Apollo nodded. "It was," he admitted. "And then, it was built again, and destroyed countless more times. You've been gone for quite a while, brother. Time passes and things change."

"But how?" Hercules persisted. "Things could not have gone so wrong!"

"Well, the war of the gods changed a lot of things."

Apollo motioned for Hercules to sit once more. "If you'd like, I can tell you a little about it."

Hercules returned to where he was sitting, and the two began to speak of what had transpired.

IV

A long, long time ago...

Zeus entered the room. Within the room, there was a table. Around the table sat five individuals, only one of which he recognized.

At the head of the table sat a hefty, bearded man, wearing a horned helmet and holding a scepter. Directly to his right sat a boy, not yet in his teens from his appearance, who wore a strange pointed hat and dressed in a long robe. On the boy's right was what looked like a cross between a bush and a man. Zeus had trouble even distinguishing a face.

On the bearded man's left sat a tall and strong-looking man with very dark skin. This man did not look very happy to be there. On that man's left sat the only person Zeus knew: Ra, the sun god of the Egyptians. He looked up as Zeus entered. From behind the hawk-eyed face, Zeus thought he saw some recognition. Considering how Alexander of Macedonia had treated Egypt, Zeus could not imagine it was good cheer.

As he approached the table, a strange chirping and clicking sound emerged from the man-bush. The Dark Man turned to Zeus, cocking one eyebrow.

"The Green Man says that you are late," he interpreted coldly.

"Yes," Zeus replied, taking the last remaining seat at the foot of the table. "I suppose I am. I was never told there was a gathering here at all, and I only just found out about it a short time ago."

The Bearded Man laughed loudly. "Do not think twice of it, newcomer. We have only just begun, after all."

"Wench," The Bearded Man snapped his fingers, and a beautiful blonde woman, with her breasts covered in metallic armaments and a pleated dress tied about her waist, rushed to his seat.

"Bring our brother something to drink," he commanded her. "He is no doubt thirsty after his journey from—"

He looked at Zeus expectantly.

"Oh!" Zeus realized the Bearded Man had about as much of an idea of Zeus' identity as Zeus had of his. "Greece. Well, Rome... or Mount Olympus, if you'd like to get specific."

"Zeus," The Dark Man sneered, identifying him.

"Yes, I am Zeus," he confirmed. Turning to his left, he greeted his hawk-headed neighbor. "How are you, Ra?"

"I am fine," Ra answered coldly. "Only a little insulted by the calling of this meeting. How are you?"

"I'm well." Zeus smiled as convincingly as possible. "A little confused, perhaps. What exactly is this?"

"This is a meeting of gods," the Bearded Man answered. "Since there are so many of us now, coming from every corner of the world, we thought it would be best to gather together and assess our dominions. I am Odin, of the Norse people. It seems you have already met Ra, the sun—"

"I can speak for myself, thank you," Ra interrupted Odin. Assuming a proud posture, he announced: "I am Ra, The Great Sun-God of Egypt."

"Should we all be impressed now?" The Dark Man mocked Ra's assertion. "Maybe sacrifice some goats, or do you prefer virgins?"

"Who are you to speak to me as such?" Ra cried insultingly at the Dark Man. "I demand respect! I am The Great Sun-God of Egypt!"

"You know, hearing it a second time does make it sound more awe-inspiring." The Dark Man turned to Zeus. "I am Ngai, god of—"

"You dare to insult me?" Ra pushed his seat back from the table and stood, placing his palms on the table surface. "You would insult Ra, The Great Sun-God of Egypt?"

"We know who you are, Ra," Odin boomed. "You do not need to keep reminding us! Now, please, be seated."

Ra reluctantly returned his chair to its position around the table.

"As I was saying," Odin resumed his role-call, pointing to the man-bush, "this gentleman does not truly have a name. He's only referred to as The Green Man."

"And this little guy next to me," Odin playfully patted the boy's head, squishing the hat a bit, "goes by the name of Merlin."

"I'm young, not little," Merlin protested, straightening the hat, only to have it flop down again. "Do not call me little."

"You are lucky to be called at all," Ngai muttered.

"I don't like this table, either," Merlin continued, ignoring the critique. "It should be round. That would more symbolize equality, wouldn't it?"

The Green Man chittered.

"The Green Man is wondering why you are even here!" Ngai translated.

"Right," Ra agreed. "You're not even a god!"

Zeus watched this interaction with some slight interest. He was still not entirely sure what was happening at this meeting. Chiron had only informed him about it this morning. He had thought it might be good to attend, since a lot of the other gods were going to be there as well. He had been expecting more Persian and Babylonian attenders, gods he was already familiar with. These gods were new. They represented peoples he had only begun to hear about recently. He was beginning to understand the world was becoming a larger place. With more cultures, there would, naturally, be more gods. Zeus knew even then it had been facetious, but he had assumed more people interacting meant he would be getting more worshipers. It only seemed natural.

"I will have you know," Merlin's pre-adolescent voice interrupted, "the day is coming when I will raise and tutor the great once and future king!"

"I should think not!" Ngai argued back.

"If there is going to be a once and future king, he's going to be from Egypt." Ra insisted.

"You don't even have kings," Ngai argued in frustration. "You have Pharaohs!"

The Green Man chattered.

"The Green Man asks you if it's going to be the Great Sun-King of Egypt," Ngai informed Ra. "He also says he not only knows the once and future king, but he knows which Celtic tribe he comes from."

"Why is it that you alone understand the Green Man?" Ra challenged Ngai. "What assurance can you give us that what you're translating is actually what he's saying?"

The Green Man grumbled.

Ngai motioned toward him, and looked at Ra. "There you go," he said.

"Enough!" Odin pounded a fist onto the tabletop, diverting all attention to himself. "This arguing is futile. We are not here to debate semantics, we are here to divide our territories."

"Oh, my brothers and I already did that," Zeus stated. "Poseidon took dominion over the sea, Hades took the Underworld, and I got the land above sea level. You all are welcome to aid me if you would like.

A god could always use helpers, especially with this expanding world."

The five sets of eyes turned to him in surprise. Odin and Ra both stifled laughter.

Zeus frowned. "What am I missing?"

"We are all leaders here, Zeus." Odin spread his arms to indicate the occupants of the room. "Each of us has our own pantheons, followers, and religions. That is what this meeting is for: to divide the world into areas of influence, where we will each have our established structures."

"Do not worry, Zeus," Ra assured him. "The world is a large place, growing larger each day. I am sure there will be enough room for all of us."

Zeus sighed. He was beginning to regret coming to this meeting.

V

Oblivion was surprisingly empty. A few Furies occupied a table in the corner, sitting and drinking their mixed drinks, sharing tales of their assorted misadventures as they accomplished their quest for retribution. At another spot, Narcissus sat, staring at his reflection in the glass of white wine with that satisfied smile of his upon his lips. Next to him sat his date, a young lady wearing hospital scrubs. A couple of maenads, Dionysus' bartenders, roamed the room, cleaning tables or refilling drinks. Save for the sound of the Furies' conversation, which was not as silent as they liked to think it was, the bar was quiet. Oblivion was very rarely quiet.

The reason for the bar's surprising lack of activity sat at the bar, which was being tended by Dionysus himself. Dionysus, dressed in a nice white shirt, black, pleated slacks, and expensive shoes, avoided the eyes of the patron at the bar as much as possible. He pretended to be cleaning his glasses or wiping the clean bar once more.

The bar-resident lowered his beer-mug with a hearty thud. "Hit me again," he demanded, his voice heavy.

Dionysus rolled his eyes as he brought the pitcher of cold beer to where the customer was sitting. He filled Zeus' mug with the golden nectar.

"Beer is really disgusting," Zeus said, raising the mug to his lips and drinking deeply. "I do not know why anyone drinks it. It's really, really not good."

Zeus negated his claim by another deep swallow.

"Dad..." Dionysus began.

"I know, I know," Zeus interrupted. "I shouldn't be drinking this much. It's not healthy or something, right? Well, I've had a rough day... I need to relax."

"Actually, I was going to tell you this is only your second beer," Dionysus said, looking his father in the eye. "There is no way you could be as intoxicated as you're trying to act. You don't need to do theatrics for me."

Zeus nodded. "Aren't you the god of theater?" he asked, as if surprised his performance was not being more appreciated.

"Yes I am," Dionysus answered, returning to his cleaning 'duties.' "That's one of the reasons I'm telling you to stop it. You can't act, Dad."

The front door opened, and Dionysus looked up expectantly. The Egyptian god, Set, peered through the door with a particularly ravishing bronze-skinned young lady on his arm. Dionysus smiled to him quickly, but when Set saw Zeus seated at the bar, he turned around and left, taking his business elsewhere. Dionysus sighed. While he loved (or at least tolerated) his father, Zeus was horrible for business.

Zeus indulged in another long drink from his mug. Dionysus moved to where his father was seated and refilled the mug before his father had time to request it.

"How could you do this to me, Dionysus?" Zeus wailed as he was refilling the mug. "How could you have kept my son here for over two thousand years? I met with you several times over these years. You could have said something. You knew how worried I was about him."

"We've been over this, Dad," Dionysus said as calmly as possible. "I had no reason to ask him to leave. Quite the opposite, actually: he and Jason were big hits around here. They even preformed a stage show once in a while. The customers seemed to really enjoy them, and that was good for business. Also, I had no reason to alert you to his prolonged presence here. In the same vein, I had no reason to alert you to his activity. If you had known, you would have come and taken him away, which could have potentially been bad for business. Also, and I hate to be childish about this, but you never asked."

Zeus shook his tired head. "I did not give you this bar so you could abduct my son," he growled.

Dionysus sighed for the umpteenth time since his father had entered. "You didn't give me this bar," he stated. "I pay for this bar with a high percentage of the finest alcohol I bring in. That's merchandise I can't sell to my customers. How is that not payment?

"Now, getting back to Hercules: once again, I did not abduct him. Hercules came here willingly. I simply did not ask him to leave and, like I've said, you have yet to give me a reason to convince me I should have. I run a bar, Dad! Bars don't function if the owner kicks out his best patrons."

"You saw how concerned I was!"

"Your emotions are not my responsibility."

Dionysus returned to the counter, wiping the invisible dust away once more. Zeus inhaled another drink.

"This stuff really is disgusting," Zeus grumbled.

"And yet, you keep drinking it," Dionysus answered without looking up.

"I sent Cupid here to look for Hercules, you know?"

"I remember." Dionysus sighed as he recalled the incident. "Don't do that again. If you get a little alcohol in him, Cupid tends to be a bit liberal with his pheromone distribution. I spent two hours, trying to peel Ares away from one of my bartenders."

"Hera's not happy about this," Zeus stated, as if it were news.

"No shock there." Dionysus looked up at his father. "Does it affect your plans at all?"

Zeus turned to look at his son quizzically. He raised his eyebrows. "Should it?"

Dionysus smirked. "I just thought I'd ask," he replied.

The two continued their interaction in relative silence. Zeus continued drinking his foul beverage, and Dionysus continued to wish he would stop soon. After all, he ran a bar. Bars don't function if the owner refuses to ask their worst customers to leave.

VI

Morpheus had never thought of himself as particularly attractive. Sure, his luxurious white mane was full-bodied and well-maintained. His skin was smooth and pale, made even more so by the hair surrounding it. His eyes were dark brown, nearly black, and as they gazed out of his pale face, those who looked into them could feel themselves being pulled into the darkness of sleep. He was on the tall side, roughly 6'1", and thin, with fair musculature. His nails were slightly long, but they were clean and well-manicured. His posture was perfect, and his gait was strong.

Morpheus had never thought of himself as particularly attractive. He knew he was, but he did not like to flaunt it. Rather, he did not like to flaunt it much.

Originally, the Land of the Dreaming, Morpheus' kingdom, had been located in the Underworld, adjacent to Hades' domain. After the gods had exiled themselves to this alternate dimension, Morpheus had relocated most of his kingdom to Olympus Prime. It made sense, since he could be in better contact with the other gods, and Zeus had more resources for his research.

After the war, many of the gods felt like they needed to be a tighter community, so they became more centrally located. Even Hephaestus, who traditionally preferred to be left alone, moved his workshop to a private area where he could work on his technological developments. Just about the only two who refused to relocate were Hades and Poseidon. Since their own kingdoms were the most vast and demonstrative, it made sense. They wanted to keep their own private realities. Poseidon had actually remained in the Earth dimension, since he had not taken much of a part in the war, and very few of his enemies had dared to challenge him. Poseidon was one of the three most powerful gods (Zeus, Hades, and himself). Of these three sons of the Titan Cronus, some would say he was the strongest. Even warring gods had known not to attack Poseidon. If they had, the ending of the war may have been much different. Also absent from Olympus, at least for the most part, was Morpheus' little sister, Thanatos. She had always been a free spirit, roaming where she chose. No one really complained about not having her as a resident on Olympus.

After Morpheus had relocated, he saw he needed to integrate himself into social circles. He had always known the gods casually, but he had never truly interacted with them, at least not on a personal level. Now that he was going to be so closely associated with them, camaraderie seemed to be a necessity. After all, if they were going to be together, it seemed to make sense they should at least be friends.

Friendship with each one of them seemed to be illogical. Morpheus was not the most social of individuals anyway, and it did not make sense for him to attempt to force a friendship with every god or goddess on Olympus. Morpheus picked out a select few to draw close to. Artemis seemed to be a logical choice. She was a moon goddess after all, and night was when he did his best work. The two of them seemed to relate on many issues as well, and Morpheus enjoyed spending time with her. She was free, or at least gave the impression of being such, and she was not as obsessed with sex as many of the others seemed to be. Being the dream lord, Morpheus was familiar with all types of sex, having seen and supplied each one in individual minds for as long as he had been working. After seeing it for so long, Morpheus had ceased to see its attraction. It was not that he objected to sex, as a rule. He simply did not believe it was everything people thought it to be.

As they walked together, Morpheus noticed that Artemis smelled nice. She generally smelled nice, so this was no surprise in and of itself, but Morpheus was especially appreciative of the scent today. She smelled like a field of lilacs, freshly lavished with rain. Morpheus had never smelled that in particular before, but he imagined it smelled something like she did now.

She was dressed in a pair of jeans, tennis shoes, and a comfortable t-shirt. He was dressed in a pair of pleated black pants, loafers, and a gray shirt. The two of them were walking together through the courtyard, talking to one another and listening to the distant sound of Apollo's guitar.

"I've been thinking," Artemis began her musing. "Do you remember how the Romans used to treat the Christians?"

"Of course I do," Morpheus nodded. "Christians were brought to the stadium to be fed to lions or simply killed for fun. That was what passed for entertainment at the time. It was sport."

"I remember," Artemis nodded, shuddering slightly. "Well, I was just considering the fate of Rome. That was really the height of their power. I mean, one could say Rome never did recover fully from the fire in Nero's time. It went from there to the Byzantine Empire, and from there to... well, what sits on Roman soil now?"

"It's not even Rome any longer." Morpheus shrugged. "I think they call it... oh, it starts with a 'v'..."

"The Vatican," Artemis finished his statement. "Rome is the Vatican now, the headquarters for the Catholic Church. After all those years where Rome slaughtered Christians, wouldn't you say the Christians... won?"

Morpheus shook his head. "That was Constantine," he said. "He was the one who brought Catholicism to the public. In my opinion, he did that as a way to control the people under one united religion, rather than the scattered individual cults, each devoted to their own deity. It was a brilliant strategy, if you think about it. Catholicism has a much more rigid design than any of our systems."

Artemis shrugged. "I was just noticing there's no more Rome, but there are still billions of Christians, dancing on the ashes of Rome's fallen empire."

"So noted." Morpheus nodded.

He began to consider what Artemis had said.

Apollo's music grew stronger and louder, the closer they got to his location. Morpheus and Artemis passed him, nodding casually to the musician. He seemed to be pretty heavily engrossed in conversation with someone. Morpheus felt as if he ought to recognize who it was, but for some reason, he could not immediately place him.

He began to consider what Cupid had said to him earlier.

Morpheus stopped dead in his tracks a few yards from where Apollo was seated. He turned to examine the conversation partner. He did know who it was!

Artemis stopped as well. "Is something wrong?" she asked, turning and following Morpheus' gaze.

"I don't know," Morpheus stammered. "Is that... is that really Hercules?"

"Yes it is." Artemis nodded. "He returned a short while ago. I'm surprised you had not heard. Hera's livid."

"I can't imagine why," Morpheus muttered sarcastically. He continued to examine the returned hero with a perplexed look.

"Morpheus," Artemis prodded him. "What's going on?"

Morpheus did not answer her. He began to consider Homer and one of his less-popular books.

VII

Hercules' head was spinning. The tales Apollo told him of the gods and their exile from the Earth-dimension were unbelievable. The war they had fought with the foreign pantheons was, at once, disturbing, startling, disappointing, and exciting. Hercules wondered if, had he not been at Oblivion, the outcome would have been different. Hera seemed to think it would have been, but it was more likely his fate would have been the same as other heroes, like Theseus, Ulysses, and Atalanta.

"So," Hercules interrupted Apollo as he stopped to take a breath, "you're telling me Aphrodite is no more?"

Apollo's eyes fell as he remembered the demise of the love goddess. "Yes," he said with despair. "Our enemies decided they needed to make an example. Aphrodite was their chosen victim. That was really the sign that Zeus chose to justify our exile, so I suppose their sign was successful."

"Did no one confront Hades?" Hercules asked. "Surely, he would have returned her. She was too important. She was an Olympian!"

Apollo shrugged. "Of course we confronted him," he answered. "He refused to comply, claiming he did not have her amongst his number. He continues to claim that."

"Then, perhaps she is not dead!" Hercules cried, grasping for hope.

Apollo looked back at him sorrowfully. "If she is not dead," he said, "then where is she? It has been so long, someone here would have known."

"Have you checked at Oblivion?"

"Well, you were there for a little while," Apollo chuckled. "Have you seen her in the past two thousand years?"

Hercules searched his brain, trying to remember anything. Discovering that he couldn't, his face fell with a sigh.

Apollo lay a hand on his shoulder. "It's been a long time," he said, trying to be comforting. "The world has moved on, Hercules. Very few even remember that we exist."

Hercules sat in silence for a moment, digesting what had just been said. He was no longer the son of the most powerful god in the universe. He was now the son of a shadow, a reflection of the past, of a world long since dead.

"So, since the exile," Hercules confronted Apollo with the question he had been wanting to ask since the conversation began, "does anyone worship us anymore?"

Apollo chuckled. "That's really what you took away from that story?"

"Well, I'm used to people paying homage to the gods of Olympus! I'm used to people giving us tribute!"

"I think Artemis and Athena still have some temples in Europe," Apollo considered the question, "but for the most part, no. No one worships us like they used to. It's really not such a big deal."

"Not a big deal?!" Hercules exploded. "We are Olympians! How could it not be a big deal?"

"Well, I'm still the God of Music," Apollo rationalized. "Nothing can change that, and having people realize it really isn't all that important. Every song written is a tribute to me. That's all a god needs. In a sense, even without people actively worshiping me, I'm doing better now than I ever have before. More people means more music, and more music means more tribute. I'm not the only one benefiting from the expanding world either. Technology is booming, so Hephaestus is satisfied. People are still growing crops and producing goods on Earth, so Demeter's not complaining. The sky, the sea, and the Underworld are still functioning, so your dad and uncles are pretty satisfied. All in all, it's a good time to be a forgotten god."

Hercules still had trouble grasping the concept. "What about people fearing us?" he continued to probe. "Do you not miss people fearing you might smite them if they fail to present a perfect sacrifice?"

"When has a human ever truly feared me, honestly?" Apollo inquired with a cocked eyebrow. "Still, I see what you're getting at, and no. Sure, Dad and a couple of us had trouble adjusting to the whole 'existing behind the curtain' concept. I still don't think Ares is too comfortable with the idea. After a while, though, most of us got used to the idea, and everything was good. There really was not much of a choice. Besides, now we don't have those pesky overachievers trying to impress us with their formulaic acts of bravery and their constant attempts to reach us. It's kind of nice, actually."

A string snapped on Apollo's guitar. He removed it, and set about restringing the instrument.

Hercules considered the ideas Apollo had just presented. It was the complete opposite of everything he had known! The gods were powerful, and they needed to be respected as such. People ought to fear them.

"I don't know if I could ever get used to that." Hercules sighed.

"Well," Apollo replied, still restringing his guitar, "I guess it's good that no one ever really sacrificed to you, isn't it?"

"I suppose," Hercules replied with a huff.

In the corner of his eye, Hercules saw Artemis walking with Morpheus. He had been surprised at how attractively she was dressed. She still looked nice. All the new forms of clothing looked more attractive, and almost seductive, when compared to the clothes they had worn back in Greece he was accustomed to seeing. The clothing was a bit less comfortable, and certainly more restrictive, but they were certainly more attractive. Artemis would never have worn such sensuous clothing in Greece.

Morpheus stopped to stare at him for a moment. Hercules nodded to him in acknowledgment. He had been getting stared at quite often since his return.

"So," Apollo began, sitting his newly strung guitar upon his knee and beginning to play once more, "how is the homecoming going?"

"It's going well," Hercules replied. "Everyone seems excited to see me, well, except for Hera, of course. I'm amazed by how different the world is, especially the people. The clothes they wear now are so much... well, they're different. The women I've seen so far are so beautiful, and their clothing is so much more... beautiful."

Apollo laughed. "Well said."

"I cannot wait to see Hebe," Hercules said, anxiously. "I can imagine she looks even more beautiful than ever! Do you know where she is?"

Apollo stopped playing, and looked at Hercules. "You haven't heard about Hebe?" he asked in surprise.

Hercules threw his hands into the air. "Why does everyone expect me to have heard everything already?" he asked loudly. "I was at Oblivion, not with a town crier!"

He then frowned. "Hey, is Artemis still a virgin?"

"I don't keep tabs on my sister's sex life." Apollo shuddered. "You shouldn't either, you sick freak! Get your mind out of the gutter. And about Hebe, I just figured that they would have told you. It seems important, what with her being your bride and all."

"What is everyone not telling me?" Hercules asked, suddenly becoming concerned. "Where is my wife?"

"Hebe is dead," Apollo said, returning his attention to his guitar. "She committed suicide a bit less than a decade after you left. Last I heard, she was with Thanatos, making her way across the river Styx to meet up with your Uncle Hades. Hades has never liked Hera all that much, so I can't imagine she's having a great time."

Hercules felt the oxygen getting pushed out of his lungs. "My wife?" he gasped. "My wife is dead?"

"Yes." Apollo nodded. "If it helps any, I don't think her death had much to do with you being gone. I think she just got tired of living, especially in exile. Maybe she just wanted a change of scenery. I guess she could have just gone to Oblivion for a while. A couple of people I know did that. She had to be dramatic, though, and she went and died. Silly Hebe."

"You are such an ass!" Hercules raged at Apollo. "Hebe's my wife! You joke as if it were nothing? She's dead, and now she's being tortured by my uncle!"

"That was just speculation," Apollo assured him.

"I have to make this right," Hercules declared. "My wife cannot have died in such a manner. I must rescue her!"

"I can only think of one method to accomplish that." Apollo shrugged. "It's not a popular method, and Hades certainly does not like it, but I've heard about its usage. Well, at least once, by Orpheus. It didn't end up too well for him, though."

"I am not Orpheus," Hercules said. "Tell me more about this plan."

Apollo set down his guitar and turned to Hercules. Hercules leaned toward him, anxious to hear the plot. As they sat and discussed the idea, Hercules became more and more nervous. As difficult and dangerous as it sounded, it may be the only way. His wife would not be allowed to simply die. Hebe was his wife, and she was his pride. His pride would never die.

CHAPTER FOUR

I

ORPHEUS WAS THOUGHT TO BE ONE OF THE PIONEERS OF civilization. It was said he aided in teaching humanity about medicine, writing, and agriculture. The Greeks of his time hailed him as chief amongst musicians and poets, giving him the name of Pindar, which means "father of songs." During his journey with the Argonauts, his skill with the lyre was invaluable, especially against the Sirens of Sirenum. He was a noble and bold hero. Unlike quite a few other heroes, he did not declare himself as such with multiple affairs.

Throughout his life, Orpheus only loved one woman, the beautiful Eurydice. The two loved each other deeply and passionately. On their wedding day, Orpheus played beautiful music and Eurydice danced, enrapturing everyone who saw. One such figure who saw her dancing was a satyr. Her dancing filled the satyr with desire. Taking up his flute, he attempted to drown out Orpheus' music with his own, hoping to claim Eurydice for himself. Eurydice saw him coming and she ran. As she ran through the meadow where she had been dancing, she stepped on a venomous snake. The snake bit her and she died, almost instantly.

Orpheus was heartbroken. Orpheus took up his lyre and expressed his emotions through song. He played music so mournful, all the nymphs wept. Their weeping caught the attention of the goddess Artemis. When she listened to Orpheus' music, she began to weep as well. Taking pity on him, she encouraged him to take his song to the Underworld. There, he could plead with Hades for the return of his wife. This had never been attempted before, and it seemed obscenely improbable. Death, after all, means death. Hades more than any other should respect that. Still, Artemis could not stand to hear such heart-wrenching music without attempting to rectify the situation.

Getting to the Underworld was not much of a trick. All one really needed was the boatman's fare. Orpheus had that, and so he arrived at the gates of the Underworld in one piece. At the gates stood Cerberus, the three-headed hound who dared anyone to attempt getting past him without justification. When Orpheus approached the gates, Cerberus growled and snarled. Orpheus played his lyre, and Cerberus fell to sleep. Orpheus just stepped over him and walked into the Underworld.

Orpheus requested an audience with Hades and his wife, Persephone. When he came into their presence, he presented his request. Hades huffed and all but denied him, almost before Orpheus had finished speaking. Something about the man interested him, though, and the fact he had worked his way this far did impress him. He asked Orpheus why his request should even be considered. Orpheus took his lyre from his shoulder and told his tale in the form of a song.

He played beautifully as he always did, with his music full of passion and his lyrics ringing with heart-felt loss. It was the song of a forsaken and bereft man, a ballad so full of sorrow and pain it has yet to be equaled to this day. When he had finished his song, he looked and saw tears flowing from Persephone's eyes and Hades' frozen expression melting. To Orpheus' surprise, Hades informed Orpheus he was permitted to retrieve his wife. Eurydice could accompany him back to the world, provided she followed him there and he not look upon her until they both had reached the banks of the river Styx.

Orpheus was so excited by the prospect of getting his bride back he agreed to the stipulation immediately. It was an odd stipulation, but he was not about to argue with Hades, thus endangering his odds of getting Eurydice back. As soon as Hades and Persephone had left to retrieve his bride, he turned his focus on the door through which he had entered and kept it there. Once they had returned with his unseen bride, he advanced toward the exit, hearing the footsteps of his love behind his own. He played Eurydice's favorite song for her as he walked. Orpheus was overjoyed to hear her voice singing along with him. Every instinct he had commanded him to turn to his bride and embrace her. He longed to assure her he had never forgotten her, that he would always love her, and nothing would ever separate them again.

The walk back to the river was the longest passage of time Orpheus had ever been forced to endure. The sound of Eurydice's voice filled him with hope as well as fear that he would do something to endanger her return with him. With his eyes glued on the path before him, Orpheus saw the banks of Styx approaching. He sped his walk a bit, eager to end the journey. Soon, the muddy bank was beneath his feet. With relief, he spun to set eyes upon his bride once more.

Eurydice had been a few steps behind him. She had not yet reached the shore. As Orpheus turned, his eyes met Eurydice's for the last time. He saw sorrow locked in them as she was stolen away, forever to return to her home in the Underworld.

If Orpheus' songs before his journey had been filled with sorrow, they seemed to be positively gleeful compared to the songs he sang afterward.

II

There is something counterproductive to the question "What's the worst that could happen?" Even considering the worst that could happen brings the possibility into reality, and the Fates sometimes take it as a challenge to think of something even worse. It is funny that the same does not apply to the phrase "this is as good as it gets." When one has accepted that it is as good as it gets, all of the other good things that could have happened tend to agree and they do not occur. At the same time, the Fates once again take notice, and they begin to think of ways to destroy the glee and cheer one may have found. It is best to avoid using either phrase in most situations, since both are "hot button" phrases definitely receiving the Fate's attention. While on the subject matter, the phrase "it doesn't get much worse than this" ought to be avoided as well. In reality, it can always get worse.

Dionysus is about to discover this.

———————

Business had not picked up much throughout the day, and Zeus had not left. It was getting pathetic, really. Dionysus had been forced to send two of his maenads home early, since there simply was not enough work to justify having them on the clock. Cthulhu, the Great Old One, had come in and taken his traditional spot at the back of the bar, where he sat with a pitcher of beer, considering which world to devour next, but that was to be expected. He came in regularly, and his presence was certainly not as disturbing as that of Zeus. After all, if no one bothered Cthulhu, Cthulhu bothered no one. If no one bothered Zeus, he was almost insulted and would begin to bother everyone. For a bar where time does not exist, it certainly seemed to be crawling slowly. Dionysus was considering the exact procedure on how to actually cut his father off, when he heard the door opening.

He looked up expectantly, as he had done every time he heard the door open. His heart was filled with horror as he saw the new arrival.

As Hera stepped through the door, Cthulhu hurriedly placed a few coins on the table and left. The two Furies who had remained at their solitary table quickly stood and vanished out the door. Dionysus shuddered and nudged Zeus, who was still heavily involved with his third beer. Zeus looked up, and then quickly returned his attention to the half-empty chaser, trying ineffectively to disappear within it himself.

"Oh, don't think that I can't see you, great father of the gods," Hera growled as she approached the bar. "Even if you were invisible, I could still smell that cheap scent you insist on wearing!"

"There's no way you could miss me, sweet love of my life." Zeus sighed. "There's practically no one else in the bar."

"There really isn't," Dionysus eagerly agreed. "Everyone seems to have better things to do. I'm willing to bet that the two of you do as well. Oh, and to be fair, the cologne isn't cheap. It just smells like it is."

Zeus rolled his eyes. "Son..."

"Hey." Dionysus stepped back defensively. "I'm just trying to be helpful. How are you, Hera?" he asked a bit sarcastically.

"Do not speak to me, you glorified barkeep," Hera snarled at him. "I am almost as angry with you as I am with him."

Taking a deep breath, Dionysus swallowed his rage. He had always thought hiring a Cyclops to be security would be a little over-the-top. At this moment, he could think of nothing he would enjoy more than seeing Hera thrown out by an enormous, slobbering monstrosity.

"I cannot stop thinking about what your son has done," Hera continued her tirade at Zeus. "Do you realize he may as well have murdered my daughter? Had he been there, he could have at least brought her some comfort, for what little comfort could be expected from your side of the family. But no! He had to neglect all of his duties and his responsibilities. He wasted so much of his life away doing what? Drinking and free-loading in this – this rat-trap!"

Dionysus finally had enough. "Get out of my bar!" Dionysus ordered the feuding couple, pointing authoritatively to the door. He could put up with degradations and insults to his person, but he would be damned before anyone was permitted to insult his exceptional establishment.

"How could he think," Hera continued, ignoring Dionysus' outburst completely, "he could just casually come back into the world as if nothing had happened, and reclaim his spot on Olympus uncontested? And you, you welcome him back with open arms! What is wrong with you? How could you allow this atrocity to go unpunished? Hebe was my daughter!"

Zeus took another drink from his beer. He looked up at Hera. "Are you quite through?"

Hera glowered back at him with unfiltered rage and nodded. She had said everything she had rehearsed. That being the case, she could think of nothing more to say.

"What would you like me to do, Hera?" Zeus asked her as calmly as possible. "Would you like me to expel him from the Mount and banish him to the Earthly domain? I can't do that. If you think the results of his absence were dire, imagine what would happen if he were present in a world he doesn't even come close to understanding. The humans on Earth have progressed, surely, but to them, Hercules is a fairy tale hero like St. George or King Arthur. They would have no idea what to do with a confused legend. I have already assured you consequences will be forthcoming, and they are."

"So you say," Hera huffed, "but where are they?"

"Hopefully at the bottom of this glass," Zeus said, holding up the half-empty mug of beer and staring into it, distractedly.

"You could always order Hercules and Jason to work here for an undetermined amount of time," Dionysus suggested. "That sure would teach them."

Both Hera and Zeus looked at the bartender cynically.

"I think I told you two to leave," Dionysus replied to the glare.

"No." Hera turned once again to her husband. "In order to be welcome on the Mount once more, he must make right what he has devastated."

"What did you have in mind?" Zeus asked, almost instantly sorry he did it.

To Dionysus' chagrin, Hera settled upon the stool next to Zeus and ordered a glass of wine. There was nothing he could do. After all, the bar was owned by Olympus, and these two ran the Mount. They were also his father and stepmother, and he did not feel right about refusing them service. Besides, as they had just displayed, they did not have to do anything they did not want to.

Dionysus poured a glass of fine Pinot Noir. If a Cyclops would be over-the-top, a fire-breathing dragon would certainly be too much for a security measure. Not one of those European ones either, one of those long, slinky Asian ones.

III

The graveyard was still cold. It had stopped raining, although the downpour of moisture had been replaced by the dew of the morning. Jason had not noticed either change. He remained where he had spent the night, lying upon Medea's grave. His chest was caked in mud and his arms were plunged into the dirt of the grave in a vain attempt to reach his lover's frozen body. The tears staining his face were now outlined as disgusting muddy rivulets streaming down his face to his chin. He had not stopped his shameless sobbing in the hours he had lain there. He had not yet cried nearly enough to forgive himself, nor had he suffered enough to justify his selfish actions. There was no point in seeking redemption, for there was no action that could appease his guilt. He had abandoned his love, and for that, he would never forgive himself.

Finding Jason was the easiest labor Hercules had ever under-taken, since there was nowhere else Jason would desire to be. As far as Hercules was concerned, Jason was still his partner and, therefore, his responsibility. As he stepped into the graveyard, he could practically feel the misery. Walking over the graves, he eventually found Medea's, and on it, he found his comrade.

"So," he mumbled nervously, "your wife didn't make it either, I see?"

Jason lifted his mud- and tear-caked face to look at the new arrival. Pain, sorrow, and rage poured from his eyes so powerfully Hercules was forced to take a step backward.

"My brother," he muttered. "You look horrible."

"Leave me, Hercules." Jason closed his eyes, returning his face to the ground. "I want to be alone with my bride. I do not wish to be bothered by anyone, least of all you."

"Why?" Hercules asked, knowing full well the reason, but pushing it to the back of his mind. "What did I do?"

"She thought I had abandoned her!" Jason cried without lifting his head from the ground. "She died alone, believing the man who claimed to love her had left her without a word of explanation. I wish to hold her again, to let her know my love for her never wavered and it never will. I wish I had at least been there, next to her, as the terrible disease wrecked her body. I wish I could tell her I had never abandoned her."

"But," Jason choked on his tears, "I did. I left her alone to die."

Hercules heard Jason's lament and, in his heart, he was moved. His sympathy, however, ranked second to his ambition and the promise of new adventure. He needed a comrade to join him on his new venture and, since Jason was the only one he could find, and since they had already gone on so many adventures together before, it made sense to ask for his companionship. Still, Jason would not be much help in his current state of disrepair.

"I understand," Hercules tried to relate to the grieving widower. "My wife died while we were gone as well."

"Oh," Jason acknowledged the statement apathetically. "Then, I suppose the biggest difference between us is I actually care."

"No," Hercules said patiently, "the difference is I'm willing to do something about it. Listen, I was talking to Apollo, and he told me what had happened to Hebe and as tragic as it was, I am determined to get her back."

"It won't work," Jason stated as he pushed himself onto his knees. "I already spoke to Thanatos. She informed me that Medea was gone, and she would not return her to me. She also refused to take me to her. There is nothing I can do."

At the mention of Thanatos, Hercules began to look around himself and the graveyard nervously. Even though he was technically immortal, Death still frightened him. All of the other gods would probably agree with him. Even if one is an ageless deity, the threat of extermination still makes one feel a bit uncomfortable. At one point, the idea had seemed impossible. Times, however, were changing.

"That may be true for Medea," Hercules said, after assuring himself Thanatos was nowhere to be found. "It's not the same for Hebe. Like I said, I was talking to Apollo, and he gave me an option I had not thought of before. You remember Orpheus, right? Well, Apollo told me about this time he—"

"Why would you want to go after Hebe?" Jason demanded, now standing upright as a macabre mess of mud, tears, and sweat. "You do not even love her!"

Hercules looked into Jason's frustrated face with his own expression of hurt. "Jason, that's not fair," he replied. "My relationship with Hebe was different than your relationship with Medea, but that doesn't make it any less of a marriage. Your relationship was based on true love, and mine was based on... well, Dad trying to shut up Hera. It was arranged, fine, but that doesn't mean I didn't come to love Hebe. I'm not going to just lie on my wife's grave; I'm going to get her back. So, if you're done feeling sorry for yourself, I could really use your help. Get yourself cleaned up, and let's get going. We have a lot of work to do."

Jason stared back into Hercules' eyes, unflinching. He was angry and he was hurt. It felt good to blame Hercules, but he knew he couldn't do that, at least not without pointing the finger back at himself. After all, they had both chosen to go to Oblivion, and they had both chosen to not leave. He wanted to hate Hercules so badly, but he could not. Hercules seemed to be the only one he could relate to.

"All right," Jason finally relented. "What are you willing to do, in order to win your wife back?"

"Anything," Hercules answered. "Which is good, because that's probably what Hades is going to demand I do."

At the mention of Hades, Jason felt an invigorating chill vibrate down his spine. He had never met Hades before. From the stories he had heard, he was glad of that. No one wanted to meet Hades. He was not even welcome on the Mount! That, of course, made the potential meeting even more intriguing.

A long, long time ago...

Hephaestus had nice hair. It hung from his head in torrents of amber brown, shining as the sun hit it. The strength and body of the hair was beyond that of a normal mortal as it flowed from atop his regal head to just below his strong jawline.

His shoulders were broad and firm, as if he were perhaps more fit to carry the globe than the titan Atlas who was punished with the task. His arms and forearms rippled with an intimidating musculature as his biceps and triceps reminded those who saw them he could tear entire worlds apart with only their strength. His deltoids made the rocks with which he worked feel like putty in comparison. His abdomen was stretched so tightly and with such definition it seemed as though one would have better luck punching their way through a brick wall than his torso. An entire army would think twice about approaching a being with a chest as rigid, firm, and broad as his was.

Dropping below the waist, however, was a different matter. His left leg was of similar make and build, with hamstrings that looked as if they could provide enough force to alter the Earth's orbit and calf muscles that looked as if they had been carved out of stone. His right leg, however, was the complete opposite. It was weak and shriveled, and it forced him to walk with a cane. Without the cane, the limp he had would have been sever enough that it would be nearly impossible for him to walk. This handicap which haunted him throughout his entire life caused him constant shame. In the eyes of many of his peers, he was perceived as useless.

Looking at his face, one often did not even notice the deep green of his eyes and how they sparkled from the emeralds shining within. One would not see the perfection of his nose, nor the fullness and natural curve of his lips. The birthmark, covering nearly all of the left side of his face, generally distracted them. The birthmark resembled a burn, and it swelled his left eye socket into a permanent squint, pulling the corner of his lips upward, as if in a sneer, and flaring his left nostril.

It was for this blemish that Hephaestus, despite his physical prowess and his otherwise attractive looks, was considered not only useless, but ugly. It was not a fair classification, but there was nothing that could be done of it. As the son of both Zeus and Hera, he ought to have been flawless. His failure to comply with this, while not his fault, could not be forgiven.

Hephaestus was the god of the kiln. Every technological and military advancement, made by the Greeks or Romans, could be traced back to him, whether directly through his production or indirectly through his influence. Hephaestus spent much of his time alone at his furnace, building prototypes for the products he was inventing or improving the designs he had already produced. Despite his exile from Olympus, the gods still came to him every time they needed anything built or developed.

Hephaestus was hard at work on something. Later, he would say he could not remember exactly what it was, but it was something very exciting. Zeus' arrival halted his development.

"Hello, son," Zeus greeted him in a voice lacking any semblance of cheer.

Hephaestus set down his tools, took hold of his cane, and used it to pivot so as to look Zeus in the eye. "Hello, father," he returned the greeting, smiling as best he could with his decrepit mouth. "What brings you to my corner of the world?"

Zeus smiled weakly. "Can a father not come to see his son without needing a reason to justify it?" he asked.

"No, a father can," Hephaestus answered, nodding, "and you are my father. However, in all the years I have been your son, you have never come to me without provocation. Unless you give me reason, I don't see why this meeting should be any different."

Zeus looked hurt for a moment. "Have I been such a poor father to you?" he asked.

Hephaestus shrugged. "You did let Mother exile me from the Mount."

He turned, resuming work on his project.

Zeus had no response to that. After all, Hepha was right. Hera had resented him from the first moment she saw his deformed leg and the blemish upon his face. When Zeus was not looking, she had dismissed him from the Mount, ordering him to never return. Hephaestus had been forced to grow up on his own, with no family to support him and two significant handicaps working against him. As he grew, he learned to compensate for his weaknesses. His skill at engineering became unmatched, as he designed new technologies. When he came of age, Zeus supplied him with his own workshop to work on his projects, as well as making him the God of the Kiln and, by consequence, technology. The workshop was near the Mount, but not on it. Hera's exile remained in place.

Zeus approached his son, laying a hand upon his shoulder. "What are you working on?" he inquired.

"It's a hammer," Hephaestus answered. "One of those new Norse gods asked me to make it for him: The one with the long, blond hair. He said he could never let anyone know he outsourced the job, so I would never get credit or thanks, but he's paying me enough, so I can ignore that. Besides, it's fun. There's going to be enough power in this thing to command thunder."

"Son, you should not be building weapons for our enemies." Zeus sighed.

"What are you talking about, Dad?" Hephaestus frowned, turning to his father. "They're not our enemies."

"Perhaps not yet." Zeus sighed again as he turned away, attempting to cover his emotions. "But they will be."

Hephaestus was not used to seeing his father like this. He turned away from his kiln. "Father," he implored, "what are you not telling me?"

"There was a meeting," Zeus replied heavily, "between the heads of the pantheons. We were dividing up our territories, deciding who would reign where, and the boundaries the other gods were not permitted to infringe. I was able to maintain dominion over Rome and some other, less significant territories, but I'm not naive. I know gods are never satisfied with only what they're given, especially not when there are others who possess similar or greater properties. I know this because I know myself. I would never allow such an infringement to stand.

"I am old, son," Zeus said as he turned to face Hephaestus again, with eyes echoing the sentiment. "We, the former Greek and current Roman gods, are old. The world has expanded, causing people groups and pantheons to intermix. This is not our world any longer. It belongs to other more expansive, less impressive individuals. They will not stop until we and what we represent have been destroyed. Power has left us."

Hephaestus looked deeply into his father's eyes. He could not remember seeing him like this, at the end of his rope. Once, Zeus had been the mighty, conquering hero, leading his family in triumph against the Titans. Now that was a story of the past. Zeus looked tired, desperate, and, to Hephaestus' surprise and horror, defeated.

"What would you like me to do?" Hephaestus asked the saddened deity before him who had formerly been the head of the gods.

"We need a weapon," Zeus answered with a slight flicker of fire reappearing behind his iris. "A new weapon. We need something so powerful and horrific it will obliterate our enemies, beyond hope of repair. We need to take a stand, declaring we will not be pushed aside. This will be our world once more, I make this declaration. Our enemies will see the Greek gods are not to be crossed or discounted."

Hephaestus nodded grimly. "I'll see what I can do," he replied in a dark voice.

Zeus nodded. "Thank you, son."

After this meeting, Zeus returned to Mount Olympus and Hephaestus returned to his kiln. He continued to work on the project for the Norse fellow. Even though his father thought it could be a weapon, it needed to get done. The big, blond guy had paid for it, after all.

IV

Hello, this is James Novus, reporting to you live. In response to the many phone calls and e-mails that you, the viewers, have sent in, demanding more information, we at the station have decided to further explore the incident now being called "The Return of the Titans." This incident occurred when two men, dressed as ancient Greek gladiators, stepped into traffic and wreaked havoc. I'm here at the site of this incident with one of the original observers. Sir, can you tell us your name please?

Um, yeah, I'm Tom Fossor. Thanks for... well, having me, I guess. What do you need to know?

Well, Mr. Fossor, you've claimed to have actually

made contact with the two "Titans." Can you tell us anything more about the encounter?

Oh, yeah, yeah, I made contact, sort of. I was walking to work from my car where I'd parked it in the lot. We need to have cheaper parking in the city, by the way. Two dollars a day is too much to pay for me just to come to work. I mean, I tried riding the bus, it smells funny all the time. Oh, we should have better laws enforcing sanitation on public transportation too. It would make this city a lot more accessible, I think, and I'm pretty sure that everyone wants that.

Mr. Fossor, if we could talk about the incident—

Well, fine, if you don't want to hear what I have to say about things people actually care about. Like I said, I was walking to work when I see these two nuts, standing on the sidewalk, like they had no idea where they were or what was going on. I actually tried to talk to one of them, seeing if he was all right. You know, I was trying to be a nice guy. That's what this city needs: more nice people.

What type of response did you get from the man you approached?

I didn't get a response. He just looked at me like I was crazy. I even complimented him on his outfit, but he just looked at me like he had no idea what I was saying! That's the problem with this world now: whenever someone takes the initiative and is actually nice to another person, the other person has no idea how to respond!

So, you didn't actually have any conversation with the individuals in question?

I think their eyes were enough communication for me. It was clear to me they just wanted human contact. Once they got it, they did not know how to respond. That could be why they went so crazy.

Are you saying you were responsible for the traffic incident?

No, no, not me: society! If people weren't so wrapped up in themselves, this never would have happened. In a sense, we're all responsible for what happened.

Well, you heard it here, folks: We're all responsible for what happened in "The Return of the Titans." This has been James Novus, reporting. After the break, we'll be back to more current headlines, specifically ones concerning celebrity advocates and equal rights for the rat population in Hamlin, Germany. You may be surprised to learn who's leading the charge. We'll be back in thirty seconds.

———

Hera and Zeus walked together, toward the nexus, through the Field of Sobriety. Neither was drunk. If at least one of them had been, the walk would have probably gone a lot faster.

"That was a nice place," Hera said. "I like nice places. I don't seem to go to those as much anymore."

Zeus stopped dead in his tracks. A cloud of impending doom settled over his head.

Hera turned to Zeus. "Why don't you ever take me anywhere nice?" she asked.

Zeus sighed, trying unsuccessfully to formulate an exit strategy. "You embarrass me, sweetheart," Zeus stated, deciding to give the honest answer. "I hate to just say it like that, but it's true."

Hera could say little to refute this. She did embarrass him; in fact, she reveled in his embarrassment.

Hera rolled her eyes, resuming her trek toward the nexus. "Well, if you didn't make it so easy," she huffed. "It certainly wouldn't happen so often. I can't embarrass you unless you do embarrassing things. Don't blame me for pointing them out."

"Honey," Zeus sighed, "I didn't mean to say that—"

Hera continued, "I would think you would appreciate me embarrassing you. At least it gives you an incentive to not do it again. Face it, without me, you'd just go around embarrassing yourself, and no one would say anything because you're the mighty Zeus. They'd all laugh at you, when you weren't looking. I'm the reason you get any respect anywhere."

"You know, why don't I take you anywhere nice?" Zeus drawled sarcastically. "I honestly don't remember."

"Why did I marry you?" Hera replied in a similar voice. "I can't seem to recall."

By that point, they had reached the nexus.

"How do we know we haven't been gone for centuries?" Hera asked Zeus as she peered into the nexus. "It only felt like a few minutes, but who knows? We could return to find Olympus destroyed completely, all because you wanted to skip out and have a drink."

"That's not how it works." Zeus shook his head. "Time still exists here, we just do not feel the effects. Or, wait, time does not exist here, but it keeps moving in the other dimension. Well, I guess that would be obvious. What I am saying is, as long as we're keeping track of the time in this dimension, we should not have a problem in the other."

Hera cocked an eyebrow. "Well, I am certainly glad we cleared that up."

Zeus sighed, motioning for Hera to go through the nexus first, chivalrously. As he watched his beautiful wife pass through, his first instinct was to turn around and run back to Oblivion.

Zeus followed Hera through the nexus a moment later.

V

Hercules had briefed Jason on what he intended to do. Jason thought the plan to storm the Underworld and demand their wives was far-fetched or, at the very least, unrealistic. The chances of it actually working were so slim they were nearly non-existent. Still, it seemed to be the only option they had. Reluctantly, Jason had agreed to accompany Hercules on this new quest. Maybe he would be able to find a better way to reunite with his wife along the way. Hercules certainly seemed to believe his wife was waiting for him to rescue her.

"So," Jason quizzed Hercules as the two of them made their way back to Olympus, "have you ever actually met your Uncle Hades?"

"Yeah." Hercules nodded. "Once. He really was not that scary. Actually, he was kind of short."

"Short people frighten me." Jason grimaced.

"Bellerophon was kind of short." Hercules chuckled.

"Bellerophon was not an Argonaut," Jason countered.

They reached the front gates of Olympus, and Jason graciously indicated for Hercules to pass through first. Hercules did so, but did not acknowledge Jason's offer. This was, after all, his home. It only made sense he would enter first.

"So, Hebe," Jason cautiously broached the subject once they had passed through the gates. "She was not your first wife, correct?"

Hercules sighed heavily, and Jason thought he saw a hint of pain in his eyes as he remembered his former family. "No," he said eventually, "she was not. I was married once before to a beautiful woman named Megara. With her, I had two sons who were both strong and handsome. I was so proud of them."

"What happened to them?" Jason asked, carefully.

"I killed them," Hercules replied bluntly, swallowing his emotions as best he could.

Jason stopped and looked at Hercules, shocked. "You killed your family?" he burst out, trying not to sound too repulsed. "Why would you do something like that?"

"It's complicated," Hercules replied, emotion slipping into his voice. "I came home from hunting one day and found three monsters in my house without my permission. I reacted as any homeowner would, and I took up arms against them. Thinking back, I should have known something was wrong when they didn't attack me first. Most monsters will do that."

"The monsters were your family?" Jason shook his head, sympathetically.

Hercules nodded. "I should have known," he choked. With a deep breath, Hercules gathered himself. "That's why I had to do my twelve labors," he continued. "I needed to make recompense for my misdeed."

"It was not really your fault, though," Jason argued. "Your vision was clouded."

"Oh, I know." Hercules nodded. "But try telling that to your in-laws. Besides, it doesn't change the fact that I killed my wife and children."

As Hercules and Jason walked through Olympus, they still received stares of disbelief from many of the residents. Jason noticed Artemis looking at him with sorrow in her eyes. She, after all, was the one who had told Jason about what had happened. Judging from Jason's filthy exterior, she no doubt had some idea of where he had been and what he had been doing.

As they walked, they passed Hestia, who looked at the two of them with surprise and disapproval. That made sense: she was the overseer of the hearth and family, which both Hercules and Jason had abandoned. Her disapproval did very little to make Jason feel worse than he already did. Jason wondered if he would ever be able to live this down. He then realized he probably would not, since he would likely never forgive himself for what he had done. This thought brought him back to the topic he was discussing with Hercules.

"So, if you truly loved Megara," Jason probed, "why did you not fight for her as aggressively as you are fighting for Hebe?"

"That's what I thought the twelve labors were for," Hercules blurted out with more emotion than he had intended. "I had thought, when I was done, Megara would come back to me! The last labor was in the Underworld, for crying aloud! But no, all they wanted was a bone from Cerberus.

"I came back to the Mount with the bone," Hercules continued, increasing in volume as his story proceeded, "with my twelve labors completed, and what did I get? A place on the Mount, a new wife, and an evil, vindictive mother-in-law-stepmom! That's not what I wanted! I wanted my Megara back!

"I wanted my wife back," Hercules concluded with a shudder.

Jason laid a filthy hand on his muscular friend's shoulder. "I'm sorry to have brought it up," he apologized.

Hercules shook his head. "It's okay," he said. "You had a right to know. We should stop talking about this now, though."

Jason nodded. "Agreed."

"Well, at the risk of sounding presumptuous," a new voice greeted them, "let me suggest a new topic."

Both Jason and Hercules turned to the new speaker. There stood a man, shorter than either of them, wearing a charcoal blazer over his gray t-shirt and blue jeans. His thick, shoulder-length brown hair hung in rivulets and curls, and his baby-blue eyes gleamed with a devious twinkle, looking slightly out of place on his cherubic face. The character lifted a burning twig to his mouth and inhaled, then exhaled the smoke from his mouth and nose. "Where in hell have you two been?" he asked, delivering his promised subject matter.

"Cupid!" Hercules exclaimed, the pain of his lost wives fading slightly at the sight of his old friend. Gripping Cupid by the armpits, he lifted the demigod up to his own level and embraced him.

"It's good to see you again!" Hercules cheered.

"Put me down, you steroid-pumping freak!" Cupid laughed, kicking his way out of Hercules' hold.

"What have you done to yourself?" Hercules critiqued Cupid as he set him on his feet once more. "You look as if you—"

"I look like I've assimilated," Cupid finished the accusation. "You, not so much."

"Did you dig yourself out of a grave?" Cupid asked, turning to Jason.

"Kind of," Jason confirmed. "It was my wife's grave, and I was—"

"Oh." Cupid's eyes fell. "Right. That would make you Jason of Iolkos, wouldn't it?"

"It would." Jason extended a grubby hand toward Cupid, who reluctantly accepted it. "You would be Eros, then?"

"Well, I'm called Cupid now," Cupid admitted. "I'm astonished to meet you, after all this time. I figured, with as long as you two have been gone, you'd be digging yourself out from the other side of the grave."

"Hey." Hercules wrinkled his nose. "You smell like ash. Why are you holding a burning stick?"

Cupid cocked an eyebrow at Hercules. "Do you really want to talk to me about stink?" he asked. "And anyway, it's not ash, it's cigar. It's good cigar too: Artero Fuente's Brick House."

"What's a cigar?" Jason asked, crinkling his own nose a bit.

"Wow, you guys have been gone awhile." Cupid took another puff from his burning stick. "Why don't you go get cleaned up, and I'll tell you all about them."

Jason paused for a moment. He remembered how repulsed he had been by beer when he had first tried it. The smell of the "cigar" Cupid held was different, and yet, it was not all together disgusting. Maybe he would give it a chance. He proceeded to the bathing chamber in order to clean himself up.

A long, long, time ago...

The gods were at war.

The others did not want to admit it, but Ares could tell. They did not respect him or his utility. Many of the Olympians forgot what a major role Ares held in the formation of society. Societies are built and destroyed by wars. Ares could feel a new age coming. It was as if a new age was trying to force itself upon the world, and it was trying to leave the Olympians behind.

This was their world. The Greeks had begun this world, and the Romans had perfected it. There was no way these foreign societies were going to come in and simply replace them. If they thought the Olympians were just going to disappear without a fight, they would find themselves sorely disappointed.

Zeus was having clandestine meetings with the foreigners as if they were friends and partners. They were dividing the world into territories, assuming the other parties would respect the treaty. That would never happen. Gods sought control, and they would never tolerate sharing control with other entities for long. That was proven eons ago when Zeus and his brothers had defeated the Titans. It had been their nature: a son replaces his father. When the father refuses to die, the son must kill his father, taking his inherited title by force.

There was no lineage here, only foreigners, attempting to expand the world. Both Greece and Rome had expanded the world through war. That had been the only way at the time. These new pantheons were attempting to expand the world through diplomacy, claiming it was the new way. It was not. It would fail. One can never expect a foreign mind to think in similar ways to one's own. Whenever two minds cannot meet, war is inevitable.

It seems someone else agreed with Ares. That "someone else" had made the first strike. They were slaughtering Greek/Roman champions. Perseus, Orion, Castor, and Pollux had disappeared completely, along with Atalanta, whom Ares had never recognized as a champion until now. The bodies of Theseus and Odysseus had practically been delivered to the Olympian gates, mangled or in pieces. Most of the gods who knew thought there was no information as to what had happened to these great warriors, but Ares had taken a moment to study the remains of corpses. Strange symbols had been burned into the smoldering flesh. Ares did not know what the symbols meant, nor did he care. He knew which culture used the symbols: the war had been started by the Celts.

Dressed in his finest armor, Ares hefted his favorite spear. This was the war to end them all, more epic than Troy. War had been coming, and Ares was prepared. Across his breastplate, he strapped two daggers. They would be easy to pull for close combat, and they *could be plunged deeply into his combatant's chest. On his hip, Ares hung his favorite sword, thirsty for the blood of his enemy. He would quench that thirst before the day was over.*

"Ares," *the small voice of Artemis called over his shoulder.* "What are you doing?"

Ares ignored her as best he could. She would never understand what needed to be done. The silly goddess of the moon had likely been the one to suggest diplomacy. For being such a glorious hunter, she was a pacifist. She made him sick.

"Oh, Merda," *Artemis swore, uncharacteristically.* "You're going to war!"

"This is not your concern, moon-goddess," *Ares snarled at her.* "War is my business! Go away, and take your diplomacy elsewhere!"

"No!" *her panicked voice cried out.* "Ares, you cannot do this! You'll ruin everything!"

"I will not sit back," *Ares shouted back,* "and allow our enemies to destroy us, not without a fight! They have drawn first blood, and this is my duty!

"It is my destiny," *he added.*

"It's not!" *Artemis wailed, placing a stilling hand upon his shoulder.* "We are searching for the violators, and they will be held responsible. You'll ruin everything if you try to do this on your own!"

Ares shrugged Artemis' hand off his shoulder. Spinning as quickly as he could in his armor, he took hold of her shoulders, gripping them tightly. Effortlessly, he lifted her slender form off the ground and pinned her against a wall. He could feel his eyes flaming with rage as he held her there.

"This is what I must do!" *he bellowed wrathfully.* "We are at war, and I will answer the call to arms! I have found the violators, and they will be destroyed. This is the way it must be!"

Pinned against the wall, Artemis began to cry. "Ares, please," *she begged.*

Ares dropped her to the ground. "Do not try to stop me," *he growled, thrusting his fist into her face, as she lay sobbing, like a child, on the ground. "This is my version of diplomacy."*

With his chin in the air, and with Artemis' violent and shuddering protests behind him, Ares stormed out of Olympus. He would do what the others were afraid to do. He would destroy their enemies without mercy.

The gods were at war.

Ares loved war.

VI

When Zeus and Hera arrived back on the Mount from Oblivion, they were still arguing. It really was no surprise, since they could argue for days to decades, never really accomplishing nor establishing anything. Finally, they would grow tired of fighting with each other (usually after they had both forgotten what the original argument was about) and they would make up. That was not likely to happen any time soon.

"I cannot believe you are suggesting this," Zeus said, shaking his head with righteous indignation. "I just had my son returned to me, and you intend to rip him away again!"

"It was because of your son that I lost my daughter!" Hera insisted. "Besides, I gave the two of you a day or so together. I thought I was being generous."

"You only gave me that day so you could concoct this scheme to tear my son away from me once more," Zeus retorted. "Had you thought of it sooner, you would have come to me quicker. This plan will most surely destroy him."

"He should have thought of that before he abandoned my daughter."

Zeus began to wonder how Hercules could have ever anticipated Hebe's suicide, and he was about to tell Hera she was being unfair, but he stopped himself. That would only escalate things, and Hera was angry enough as it was.

"Go into the throne room," Zeus instructed Hera. "I will find my son and bring him there. I promise not to tell him of the plan until we're in the throne room, so you may see the dismay on his face."

"That's all I ask," Hera huffed, turned on her heels, and headed toward the aforementioned room.

Zeus watched her walk away, reluctant to proceed with what he knew needed to be done. The most likely scenario ended with both his son and, more than likely, Jason dead, and Hebe no closer to life than she had been prior to the endeavor. The least likely outcome ended with all three of the parties surviving, likely trapped in the Underworld, since his brother would never allow them to leave. Once he started allowing the formerly dead to walk again, he might just as well replace the gates to the Underworld with a revolving door, substituting a chihuahua with a spiked collar in place of Cerberus.

Zeus knew his brother, and Hades would never let that happen.

Finding Hercules was not all that difficult. With the mostly-pleasant scents permeating Olympus, the smell of cigar smoke (even good ones) was obvious. While cigars were Cupid's signature, the deep-throat laughter was unmistakable. Zeus followed it to where the three responsible parties were sitting.

Cupid looked up at him with a slightly guilty smile. "Hey Zeus," he greeted the father god. "How's it going?"

Without returning the smile, Zeus nodded back at him.

"Hey Dad," Hercules said with a wide smile and a cigar hanging out of his mouth. "Cupid's showing us how to smoke. It's a lot of fun. Do you want to try?"

Zeus thought back to his experience with cigars and the nausea that followed. He shook his head. "Smoking really isn't for me," he admitted.

Cupid laughed. "Yeah," he agreed. "Zeus' first cigar was a pretty potent one, way back in the early days. I remember the first puff; he inhaled the entire thing. You should have seen it! His face turned the color of avocados!"

"Oh, dad." Hercules frowned at Zeus sympathetically. "You can't inhale cigars."

Zeus bit back his first instinct, which was to snap at Hercules, telling him he could do whatever he wanted. Thinking back at the experience, however, Hercules was only offering sage advice.

"Yes," Cupid replied with a wry grin, "he discovered as much."

"Don't worry, Zeus," Jason, who was sitting with Cupid and Hercules, said sympathetically. "I'm not into smoking either. It really does not make much sense to me, intentionally doing something which will not only make you smell like ash, but could potentially do harm to your body."

"I am a god, Jason," Zeus said, turning to the speaker. "I have no fear for my body's condition. After all, if the Titans could not defeat me, I doubt a cigar would do me in."

"You haven't tried my Cains." Cupid smirked.

Zeus sighed. "Son," he said, turning once more to Hercules, "may I have a word with you?"

Hercules took a not-so-insulate puff on his cigar. "Well, I'm kind of spending time with Cupid, Dad," he replied. "Can you wait a few? I want to finish my cigar."

Zeus shook his head. "This is important," he answered with a heavy voice.

Cupid looked up and saw the anguish in Zeus' face. He reached his hand out and took the cigar from Hercules' hand. "Don't worry, brother," he said. "I have plenty of cigars. I think you had better go with your father."

Hercules reached out to take his cigar back from Cupid, but the god of allure shook his head. With reluctance, Hercules rose.

"Does this have to do with those consequences you were talking about?" Hercules asked. "If it does, then there's something I need to talk to you about too."

Zeus dropped his gaze. "Come with me," he said, nodding toward the throne room. The two of them walked away, Zeus with a heavy head, and Hercules following, seeming like a man walking to the gallows.

Jason and Cupid watched as they walked away.

"Wow." Jason raised his eyebrows. "I wonder what's going on."

Cupid sucked the last of his cigar in a final inhalation, extinguishing it before beginning on what remained of Hercules'. "Whatever it is," he said, after emitting a circle of smoke, "I'd bet it has to do with Hera, some consequences, and probably a long and nasty trial. He messed up pretty bad this time. This will probably make his other trials look like child's play."

"Should I go with him?" Jason asked, hoping the answer would be no. "I mean, I'm at least partially responsible for getting Hercules into this mess."

"You're completely responsible," Cupid agreed. "However, you're not Zeus' son, and Hera doesn't hate you. I think you've got a free pass for this one. I'd take it."

Jason continued to look in the direction Hercules had walked off. He hoped the trial would not take too long. After all, they needed to get started on the quest Hercules had proposed as soon as possible. However, judging from Hera's reputation, she would likely not be satisfied until Hercules was nothing more than a smoldering pile of ash, similar to what was sitting in the tray before Cupid.

"I have a bad feeling about this," he said.

VII

As Hercules entered the throne room, he saw the smirk on Hera's face as she sat on her throne, next to Zeus'. She was grinning as if she had already defeated him. It was at that time Hercules knew what they were about to discuss was likely not going to work in his favor. Zeus would either banish him from the Mount or give him some ridiculous task to appease her. That seemed to be her motif, making him do profoundly impossible labors in order to make sure he would never gain acceptance on the Mount. He had not even been back for a full day and night, and already she was trying to get rid of him (never mind she had already been rid of him for over two thousand years).

On the converse, Hercules always completed the tasks she set before him, which seemed to make her angrier and goad her into trying to think of even more difficult tasks to set before him. Hercules only hoped they would allow him to perform the labor he was intending to take part in, on his own, before they kicked him out completely. His honor needed to be restored. Plus, he felt a little guilty for Hebe's current predicament, seeing as how it was probably his fault.

Zeus advanced into the throne room. Hera's wicked smile widened slightly as he paused before turning and sitting down. Hercules stood where he had been a few hours ago, before the throne. He kept as stoic a face as possible as his father looked down on him.

"Son." Zeus sighed. "I have called you in here to deal with those consequences we had mentioned earlier."

Hercules nodded. "I've actually been thinking a lot about those myself. I understand what I did was a mistake. Look how much has gone wrong since I've been gone!"

"Let your father speak, Hercules," Hera snarled at him.

Zeus set his hand on Hera's arm to keep her wrath at bay. He wanted to hear what Hercules was saying. It gave him a few more minutes before he told his son he was sending him to his death.

"I know I can't make up for everything that happened while I was gone," Hercules continued, as if Hera had never spoken, "but I can try to make things right, while I'm here. Maybe, in time, I'll be able to make up for what I missed."

"You missed an entire war!" Hera raged. "We are barely existing, in our own alien world now, because of you!"

"You can't seriously blame the entire war's outcome on me." Hercules raised his eyebrows.

"I can, and I will!" Hera snapped. "Don't you dare tell me what I can and cannot do! Because of you, I am now without a daughter!"

"Your daughter did not die in the war," Zeus corrected her, attempting to settle his bride.

"The details do not matter!" Hera continued her rampage. "My daughter, who graciously agreed to be joined to this useless hunk of man-shaped flesh, is dead now because of his absence. He does not deserve to even speak her name!"

"I agree," Hercules dared to raise his voice again. It was not as if he could argue with any of the accusations being brought against him. He had abandoned his responsibilities, and the outcome had hurt those who were most important to him, including Jason, his best friend.

"I acted stupidly and without honor," Hercules continued, "and, while I believe I have said it already, it will take some time for my honor to be restored. I understand I have much to answer for, but before I am crucified, I would ask that I be allowed to make one last journey, in an attempt to re-establish, at least in part, the honor which I have abandoned.

"Apollo has told me the story of Orpheus, my friend and fellow Argonaut, and his bride. In the story, it is said Orpheus loved his wife so much, he took his lyre to the Underworld in order to retrieve her."

"You, no doubt, know the end of the story," Zeus interrupted him. "How Orpheus ultimately failed in his quest, and how she was torn from him a second time?"

"Orpheus did not fail to retrieve her," Hercules corrected his father carefully. "He was able to convince Hades to return her, and what he failed in was a minor detail. The convincing process is what I am concerned with. This proves Hades and Persephone can be swayed. That being the case, and with your permission, I would like to go to the Underworld, in order to petition the return of Hebe."

Zeus and Hera looked at each other in surprise.

"That's quite a proposition, son," Zeus said, returning his gaze to Hercules. "You do realize you will likely fail. Hades cannot simply allow one who has died to return to the world."

"It is not unheard of, though," Hera defended Hercules' suggestion. "While he will likely fail, there is a small chance he will succeed. I like this plan."

Hercules frowned with confusion at Hera. This may have been the first time she had ever expressed anything other than contempt toward him. For her to say she agreed with him on the subject probably meant it was a bad idea. Still, it was his duty, and his honor that needed to be restored. This was the only way he could think to do it.

"Very well." Zeus nodded. "You shall be allowed to make this journey. Will you be going alone?"

Hercules shook his head. "Jason has agreed to accompany me."

"Now, hold on a second—" Hera objected.

"That is acceptable," Zeus interrupted her, laying a cautionary hand on her arm again. "After all, he needs to restore his honor, just as you are. The two of you will leave immediately, then?"

"I would like to consult the Oracle of Delphi first to see if she has any advice for me. Right after that, we'll be gone."

Zeus nodded. "Very good, son," he said. "I admire your bravery and dedication. You have my blessing. Go forth and succeed."

Hercules began to turn in order to leave. He stopped mid-turn and looked back at his father. "What about those consequences you had just been talking about?" he asked. "Did you want to talk about them now?"

"Oh!" Zeus remembered himself. "Oh, yes, the consequences. I believe we can hold that discussion after your quest. It is meaningless to hold it prior, since these consequences now hang on the outcome of your journey."

"You're hurting my arm," Hera muttered to Zeus, referring to the tightening grip.

Hercules looked at his father, curious. He had never known his father to put aside his own agenda for the sake of another. Still, he was not about to question the verdict. He bowed appreciatively to both Zeus and Hera, turned, and left the throne room quickly before his father could reconsider his generosity.

When he was gone, Zeus released Hera's arm.

"You know," Hera said, rubbing the area Zeus had taken hold of, "if this turns black-and-blue, the others may begin to think you abused me."

Zeus shrugged. "Half of them already think you abuse me," he replied. "I doubt anyone would mention it."

"Also," Hera continued, "the fact Hercules chose the exact recompense we were planning for him on his own alleviates the punishment. It is not truly punishment if he chooses the quest willingly."

"If he fails, then you will be rid of my son," Zeus retorted. "If he succeeds, then you will have your daughter back. The fact he chose the quest out of nobility rather than requirement means nothing. The end result will be the same."

Hera slumped back in her throne, sulking. "I never expected that," she admitted. "Your son has taken responsibility for his actions."

Zeus smiled. "Perhaps he will surprise you even more in the future," he said.

"Perhaps he will die in the pits of Tartarus," Hera could not resist countering.

"Perhaps he won't," Zeus said, refusing to let his wife's negativity bring him down. He was proud of how his son had handled things. It gave him renewed hope for how things might turn out.

Still, it all depended on Hercules completing a particularly daunting task.

CHAPTER FIVE

I

HEBE WAS ASLEEP. SHE WAS GOOD AT SLEEPING, AND SHE ENJOYED *doing it, often for many hours at a time.*

Between Zeus and Hera, Hera was absolutely the more faithful of the two. Still, she had been known to have an affair every once in a while. It was commonplace on the Mount, and almost anticipated. So much so, in fact, that Hebe doubted the purpose of marriage at all. After all, with so much spousal infidelity, why even bother to get married? Was it only for appearance or social standing? Perhaps it was to make one more desirable to the opposite gender. After all, one always desires what they cannot have, especially if someone else has that thing already.

Hebe was the product of an affair, of course, so she could not be too bitter about them.

She had been declared the goddess of youth, not a bad position to hold. A lot of people enjoyed staying young for as long as they could, so she was able to gain a large mass of followers. She knew this probably was not her mother's intent when she had been appointed to this posi-

tion, but it was an obvious eventuality. Being the goddess of youth did not require a whole lot of responsibility. After all, people wanted to remain young, and they enjoyed making additional young ones to replace the youth they no longer had. It was not the most stimulating of positions, but it was a valued one, to be sure.

In addition to being the goddess of youth, Hebe had been appointed as the cup bearer to the gods, specifically to the Olympians. This position required a bit more dedication, since not only did she have to make sure she did not spill the wine (which meant she could not partake in much of it), but she had to make sure the wine was not poisoned. Zeus had assured her this was a prestigious position, and she should feel honored to hold it. All Hebe knew was that, every time she was serving the gods wine, she was at risk of being poisoned.

When she had been asked to be Hercules' bride, it was another "honor." At least, that was how it was supposed to appear. This demigod, who her mother had been trying to be rid of for so long, was now going to be her husband. At first, she had been hesitant, but after thinking about the situation, she concluded that it would be a chance to gain a little bit more notoriety on the Mount. Hercules was, after all, Zeus' favored son. She would certainly not just be a cup bearer any longer. She would go from Zeus' stepdaughter to his daughter-in-law, and Hercules would become Hera's son-in-law as opposed to her bane. The arrangement seemed to work out for both of them. Besides, it was not as if he was an unattractive man. Hebe remembered how repulsed Aphrodite had been when she had been asked to wed Hephaestus, for political reasons. Hephaestus was not a bad person, he simply was not attractive. As far as arrangements go, Hebe actually did pretty well. Love had never entered in to the equation. Love came later.

Hercules had turned out to be an incredible lover and a worthy husband. Hebe soon found herself falling in love with him. Although he claimed to, Hebe could never be sure if Hercules felt the same way about her. After all, Zeus and Hera claimed to love each other, but if the love were true, why did they feel the need to constantly challenge it with the random affairs they had? Hebe never understood it, but *perhaps she did not truly need to. After all, it was not her relationship. She only knew she loved Hercules, and Hercules claimed to love her. He demonstrated his love in many ways, chief among them, by not having affairs. As far as she could tell, he had been entirely faithful to her.*

The first few years of his absence had been difficult. She had tried to tell herself he was simply on a quest, perhaps with the Argonauts, and he had simply forgotten to tell her about it. That was something he would do, after all. Besides, Jason of the Golden Fleece was missing as well, more evidence of her theory. None of the other Argonauts were, but Hebe assumed they did not need to be. After all, Hercules and Jason were the ones with the biggest notoriety. They should have brought Orpheus to document their adventures in song, but he was so beat up after he failed to bring his wife back from Hades, perhaps he had refused to go along. This was what Hebe chose to believe.

The years became a decade, and her belief faltered a bit. Her mother had taken to ridiculing and chastising her husband for running away and not being worthy of a wife. Hebe knew in her heart her mother's accusations were untrue. However, it still hurt, especially since her husband was not there to refute the charges.

The decades had become a century, and Hebe tried to forget about Hercules. It did not happen. Hercules had been a good and faithful husband, and she had failed him as a wife. He had left her, and she would likely never see him again.

Hebe was asleep. She enjoyed sleep, and it was something she did well. While she slept, she did not have to think about the things at which she had failed.

While she slept, she dreamed. Hera appeared before her, and Hebe felt a mixture of pleasure in seeing her mother and caution at the look on her mother's face.

"Look at you," *Hera had growled,* "wasting your life away, just sleeping. You could have done so much more! You did not have to be such a waste of time and space!"

Hebe was shocked! That did not sound like her. Hera had always been supportive and, even in her criticism, at least somewhat encouraging toward her. Why was she attacking her now?

"I should never have given birth to you," *Hera continued relentlessly.* "If I had known what a disappointment you would turn out to be, I would have aborted you. I would have taken you to Hephaestus' furnace and, while his back was turned, I would have thrown you into the fire."

Hebe opened her mouth to plead with her mother to stop. She wanted to cry and ask Hera why she was being so cruel. She wanted to scream and beg her mother to stop. She opened her mouth to do these things, but found she was unable. Her mouth closed once more in astonished dismay. She was unable to make a sound.

"You're worthless," *Hera proclaimed, stepping closer and straight into Hebe's face.* "You have no value and no place amongst the gods. You would do us all a favor by killing yourself. That, at least, would save us the chore of banishing you from the Mount. You have no purpose here. There's no point to you even being here! Why don't you just kill yourself?"

Hebe's dream eyes widened, and she realized her mother was saying all the things Hebe had been afraid to think of while she was awake. They were exaggerated, of course, but Hebe had always suspected these were things that the other gods thought of her. There was nothing left for her. The tears that refused to come burned in her ducts. She felt herself listening to what her mother was saying and finding logic in it. Maybe she ought to simply kill herself, thus eliminating the duty of banishment. That was surely the only logical choice left to her.

"Look at me," *Hera continued, and Hebe could practically smell the ash on her breath.* "I am a good wife! My husband would never abandon me, for I am a good wife! You are worthless, even as a companion! Your husband left you—you are a disappointment, even in marriage. He was a good husband to you, and you have failed him as a bride. You are nothing, and that is all you will ever be. Kill yourself!"

Something clicked in Hebe's mind. Her mother, while hesitantly accepting of Hercules, would never have praised him. There was something wrong with this entire transaction.

Slowly, Hebe realized she was having a dream.

Fighting back the fear, which the creature pretending to be her mother was inducing in her, she opened her mouth once more. "Who are you?" she choked, using all of her strength to do so.

The monster in the form of her mother looked back at her, startled. It recovered quickly. "I am your mother," the creature snarled, "as much as I hate to admit it."

"You are not my mother," Hebe retorted, feeling some of her strength returning. "My mother would not speak to me like this. I know you are not my mother. Who are you?"

The creature began to appear less and less like her mother the more she resisted. Hebe tried desperately to awaken, but she could not. The dream persisted, growing perhaps stronger, now that she had identified it. The Hera-guise slipped even further, and now Hebe could see through it. She almost wished it had remained as her mother.

The creature appeared as a mass of black smoke. The stench of sulfur emanated from it as its disgusting black tentacles reached for her, swirling their way around her body, trying to enter any available orifice. It permeated through her nostrils, beat at the boundaries of her eyeballs, and crept into her ears. Hebe clenched her mouth closed even though the smoke pried at it relentlessly.

"I am tragedy," the creature snarled, and Hebe heard the voice in her mind, as if the smoke had reached there as well. "I am the destroyer. I am what you fear and I am what you have lost."

The blood flushed out of Hebe's face as the smoke crept into her garments, fondling and groping her viciously. As the violation became stronger, she began to feel her strength evaporate, as if this monster were draining it out of her, simply through contact with her flesh.

"I am your nightmare," the beast thundered in her head. "I am all the things you have ever feared, coming to feed upon your mind.

THE TIME AFTER OBLIVION

There is no safety to hide within, and no shelter to protect you from me. I am the darkness, and you are mine."

"Leave me!" *Hebe cried in desperation. At the moment her mouth opened, even the slightest bit, the smoke plunged itself through the gap between her lips. Realizing her mistake, Hebe screamed loudly, hoping the scream would awaken her. It failed. Hebe continued to scream as the beast clawed at her, shredding her garments, and tearing at her flesh.*

"Scream, child," *the beast encouraged her, mockingly.* "No one will hear you. Scream all you want. You belong to me."

The creature savaged her, slipping through her skin and into her body. It seemed to Hebe that the more she screamed, the stronger this violation became. Whenever she stopped screaming, she could feel her emotions pulsing from within her, begging to be released. There was nothing she could do to prevent this attack. Hebe felt herself slipping into the monster's grip.

II

Persephone was beautiful. Anyone who saw her would agree.

> *You are beautiful Persephone*
> *whose lovely image shines.*
> *Bring light into the darkest hour,*
> *uplift me time from time.*

Her blond hair flowed like satin, resting softly upon her strong, nimble shoulders. Her long, luxurious lashes, extending from her eyelids, framed the delicate blue paintings locked within her irises. Her pouty, full lips were naturally a deep crimson. One could hear the birds singing a bit louder and feel the sun shining a bit brighter each time she chose to curl them into a generous smile.

> *Wherever you walk, the flowers bloom*

and where you dance, birds sing.
Whenever you choose to speak a word,
new life it seems to bring.

Her skin was both fair and flawless, like a soft cream covering her body from head to toe. No freckle, mole, or dimple would mar such a pristine canvas. Many strangers would stop and watch this beautiful wonder as she walked, making the gait seem almost like a dance. Her full and firm breasts would bounce slightly with each move of her graceful hips. Her slender thighs caused her to flow like velvet across the terrain.

I swim in the ocean of your hair
I drown in your blue eyes.
I dance to the music from your lips
as you sing beaut'ful lies.

She was the daughter of Demeter, the great goddess of the hearth. Demeter was very protective of her daughter, valuing her above any within her domain. Many men, both human and god, had attempted to court and woo the exotic Persephone, yet all had failed to gain permission from her mother. Those who had proceeded with the courtship, counter to Demeter's will, learned quickly that it was a bad idea. She took it very personally.

I am not worthy to gaze upon
you and all your beauty.
You would do me honor, if only you would
nod or smile at me.

One day, while Persephone was among the flowers in a field not far from her mother's home, the Earth before her opened. Hades, the great god of the Underworld, came forth and abducted her. He had been watching her for some time and convinced himself she was the only woman he could ever be satisfied with. Persephone screamed and resisted as best she could, but Hades' hold upon her could not be broken. Hades brought her with him, back into the Underworld.

Demeter had not known of Hades' plan, and she had no idea what happened to her daughter. In a panic, she began to search the world for her. Demeter's search consumed her, and her hold on the planet's balance began to lapse. Seasons became distorted, and drought blighted the Earth, followed by a cold and merciless winter. Humans suffered, and Demeter grew no closer to discovering her daughter's location. The Earth began to die. Finally, Zeus saw he had to intervene. At first, he had viewed the abduction as a personal matter between Hades and Demeter, but it was becoming a problem for the rest of the world as well. Zeus went to his brother and asked he return Persephone to her mother.

Hades was not heartless, no matter what the other gods would say. He had seen the trials of Earth, and he had been moved. Still, in his time with his captive bride, he had grown to love her, and he had never felt as satisfied as he did when he was with her. He made a deal with Zeus: If Persephone had eaten nothing in all of her time in the Underworld, she would be permitted to return. Zeus found this acceptable.

After his meeting with Zeus, Hades approached Persephone. He knew she had not eaten anything since she had entered his kingdom. While eating was not required in the Underworld, the desire for food was not diminished. Persephone watched her captor approach. He set a bowl of twelve figs down before her. Hades explained the situation to her. He told her if she wished to return to her mother, he would accept it. All she would need to do was eat the figs. If she wished to stay with him, leave the bowl untouched. Hades left her to make her decision.

When Hades returned later, he found that only half of the figs had been eaten.

You are beautiful Persephone.

I try, but cannot see
any way, in Earth or in sky, that
you could ever love me.

III

Hades had never sold his stock in Macintosh computers. Even through the great uprising of Microsoft, he had held on. No matter how dark Macintosh's future looked, Hades had held on to the stock. That was mostly because he did not feel like selling, since it would have required extra effort. Hades was busy running the Underworld, so he usually tried to avoid any extra effort. Anyway, it was all working out now. He loved his Mac laptop; it was cool, slim, and compact. The spreadsheets also made keeping track of the Underworld residents easier.

The Underworld influx had slowed recently, over the past few centuries or so. Before, it had been restricted to deceased Greeks, Romans, and the random few others who followed the gods. Now, while the parameters were the same, very few actually came to Hades' division of the Underworld. Since less and less people worshiped the old gods, fewer and fewer gained acceptance (or were damned to, depending on the case) into the Underworld. With more time on his hands, Hades was able to be more creative with the tortures of Tartarus and the comforts of the Elysian Fields. A short time ago, maybe a century or two, he had hired a troupe of Fire Golems to patrol Tartarus, like a sadistic "police force." Around the same time, Hades had drafted a group of dryads from Artemis and stationed them within the Elysian Fields to service the residents there. The computer allowed him to record and document everything occurring in both locations. Ruling the Underworld had never been easier.

Hades sat at his computer this particular evening, studying the day's activities. Things were going perfectly well in Elysian Fields, but very, very poorly in Tartarus. This was just as it should have been.

Behind him, Hades heard his office door open. A smile spread across his lips as a sweet scent filled the room, letting him know who was standing there.

"Sweetie," came the musical voice of Persephone, "have you seen my nightgown?"

"Which one, babe?" Hades did not bother to look away from his computer. "You have quite a few."

Of course, it did not matter which one it was, since he had no idea where any of them were.

"Oh, the soft blue one," Persephone answered, "with the silk and lace?"

"The blue silk one?" Hades jerked to awareness in surprise. "I love the blue silk one! You lost it?"

Hades turned his horrified face to see his wife standing in the doorway. A sly smile played across her face, as she twirled slightly, showing off the very garment she had been asking about. Lace bands supported the outfit, seductively allowing the neckline to dip, almost a bit too deeply. The silk flowed from her shoulders, covering her body delicately like a transparent waterfall, ending at her upper thigh and displaying her strong, nimble legs.

Persephone giggled as she entered the office, planting herself upon her husband's lap and straddling him. "No, silly," she cooed into his ear. "I was just wondering if you had seen it."

Persephone pressed her lips against Hades', and the sweet wine of her breath filled his mouth. Their tongues danced together in an exotic salsa lifting them from the Underworld into the clouds. Hades gently massaged Persephone's softly heaving shoulders, and her nails dug into his back as the two enraptured each other. Time stopped and turned away, allowing the lovers a bit of privacy.

Persephone reluctantly ended the kiss and laid her head upon her husband's shoulder. "Are you busy?" she whispered, taking his earlobe between her teeth.

Hades carefully brought himself back from the ecstasy of the moment. "I just have a few things to wrap up here," he answered. "Did you need something?"

"I need you," Persephone answered, wiggling anxiously in his lap. "I'll be going back to be with my mother again soon, and I'll miss you. I just wanted to play with you for a bit."

"You know, you're a fully grown woman now," Hades said, attempting to return his mind to his work rather than the pelvis pressing into his thighs. "You no longer need to live by your mother's rules."

"Oh, but my mother still looks out for the Earth," Persephone pouted. "If I don't come back, she'll be sad and the planet would suffer. Mortals might die, you know?"

"How is that your concern?" Hades asked, lifting her face to his own again.

Once more, the two lost themselves in a kiss breaking the boundaries of form. The two bodies ceased to be, leaving only the one entity, complete and satisfied with itself.

Sliding off of his lap, Persephone ran a coaxing hand down her husband's face. "Come play with me," she begged.

With a sigh, Hades relented. He turned off his computer and stood from his chair, taking his wife in his arms.

"In a moment," he said. "Come with me and check on our favorite prisoner."

Arm-in-arm, the two of them left the room.

IV

Blood.

There was blood everywhere, dripping from her bare legs, leaking down her naked torso, covering the flesh of her arms, and saturating her hair.

The steely scent flooded what remained of her sense of smell. She knew it was her own, and there was a lot of it. Her mind numbed as she thought about how it had come to be there. This was the only reality she knew. It was the only scent she could remember.

Her wrists were bound behind her to a spike... a post, a tether, a wall... and she could not get them free. Perhaps they were broken. Perhaps they were no longer there at all. Perhaps she had been here so long she just accepted this as her only position.

There were dogs. She could see them and hear them snarling at her. She could feel them nipping at her flesh as they lunged for her body. They did so constantly, never tiring and never resting. They always failed to sink teeth into her muscle, but not her skin. Their savage teeth always nicked her flesh, barely reaching her, but penetrating just enough to leave a mark, a fresh blood stain, a new enhancement. The dogs had tethers and leashes of their own, preventing them from reaching her body, beyond the skin barrier. She was thankful for the leashes and the protection they provided. She hated the leashes for the protection they provided. Often, she wished one of them would break. That way, one of the dogs could reach her and accomplish what it was trying to do.

That would never happen.

This was reality.

It was the only reality she could remember.

V

Hades and Persephone watched the scene. Hebe was chained to a metal pole, surrounded by the savage hounds. The hounds were chained at a distance far enough away to avoid inflicting any real damage. Superficial wounds covered most of her body. Hebe was able to avoid some of the attacks by clinging to the pole, but usually the dodge attempt would only put her in the path of another dog's lunge.

She had stopped the constant screaming a long time ago, somewhat to Hades' dismay. She still screamed, but only occasionally. Prometheus did the same thing, after a time. It only meant they had accepted their fate and given up hope. That was Hades' objective, but the screaming gave him a macabre sense of satisfaction.

Laying his hand upon Persephone's shoulder, Hades pointed to the pole. "I was thinking of installing an electrical charge," he said. "That way, each time she touches the pole, she'd get shocked."

Persephone raised her eyebrows as she looked at her husband. "You're sick," she stated.

Hades shrugged. "I just don't want to be too predictable."

Persephone had always been impressed by her husband's dedication to his craft. At times, it frightened her, but at least he got the job done. There was never a shortage of horrors to be inflicted, and Hades was always looking for new ones. Persephone could ignore the lingering unease Hades' penchant for torture gave her. She loved him so much. That, alone, was reason enough to keep her love strong.

VI

Good evening everyone, I'm James Novus. Most of you are familiar with the story, jokingly entitled "The Return of the Titans," which we have been covering for you over the past month. Our investigative journalism has uncovered a potential explanation.

I'm sitting here with Mr. Fred Thomas, codenamed "Scarecrow." He is the head of a local chapter of actors who are involved in a pretty intense game called LARP. How are you today, Scarecrow?

I'm well, thank you, James. First thing I think I should say is that LARP is not exactly a game. It stands for Live Action Role Play, so it's more of a genre than a game. The players will take on the persona of a character they create, much like a film or stage actor, and perform tasks in that personality. There are a variety of settings the characters can place themselves in, within the game, ranging from medieval to modern or even futuristic.

So, you think the characters in the street were playing this game?

Again, LARP is not a game in itself, it's a type of game. What I am saying is that some of the LARPers may have gotten carried away with their characters, and the game may have gotten out of hand.

Does LARP encourage the use of drugs in any performance-enhancing activity?

Well, I cannot speak for every participant in a LARP, but I can say that I have never encouraged my group to take drugs, and I myself have never participated in a group which did. I am not familiar with the game these characters were playing, but they seem to me to be very dedicated to their craft, even to the extent of speaking an ancient form of Greek. While I do not endorse their actions, I applaud their perfection.

So, are you saying you are a Titans-sympathizer?

No, that's not what I said. I said they were very good at staying in character.

Does the game of LARP encourage acts of civil mayhem and destruction?

LARP isn't a game, it's a type of game! And, no, we don't encourage players to break the law. Look, all I was saying was that these "Titans," as you call them, may have been acting out a LARP-sequence. I don't know anything more.

Thank you, Scarecrow, that seems to—

Feel free to call me Mr. Thomas.

—bring the situation into a new light. These so-called Titans may have only been participants in the underground cult game of LARP—

Stop calling it a game! And who said it was a cult?

We'll have more details on the society and other followers of LARP as they arise. Up next, which celebrity's fashion *faux pas* may be setting a trend with a

certain sect of religious extremists in Arizona? We'll have more after these commercials.

———————

Morpheus walked purposefully toward the Olympus library. Ever since he had seen Hercules, something had been eating at the back of his mind. He needed to study.

The poet Homer had been accepted as a historic scribe in regards to the workings of the gods. Of course, humans had no solid proof that Homer had ever existed, but that did not seem to matter as much as his contributions to literature. His documentation of the Trojan War was considered unparalleled, as was his recounting of Odysseus' voyage home, and the circumstances surrounding it. These were two of the books the public got to see. Homer, who had actually been a real person, wrote many more. Zeus kept them hidden from the public as many of them might have allowed too much information into the gods and the politics of Olympus. Zeus had gone to extents to remove any evidence of Homer's existence, but the power of the written word had proven stronger even than the power of Olympus. Once something is written, it cannot be erased.

Morpheus had known Homer. He wondered if people would embrace his works so warmly, had they known who, or what, he actually was.

There was one book Morpheus was particularly concerned with at this moment: Homer's *Posterus*. Within it, Homer had predicted the future of the gods, inspired by an otherworldly insight that had driven him mad in the end. Morpheus had only read it through once, and he had found the prophecies, if they could be called that, far too obscure and vague to be anything useful. However, there had been a certain passage concerning him now.

Morpheus noticed Cupid, accompanied by Artemis, approaching him. He lowered his head to avoid their looks, but failed.

"So," Cupid called to him as they neared each other, "was I

talking to Hercules earlier, or did I just imagine that as well?"

"Now, Cupid," Artemis chided him, "in his defense, Hercules' return did seem a bit unlikely. Do not be too rough with him."

"No, no," Morpheus brushed off Artemis' sympathy, "he's right. I mocked him for saying Hercules had returned, and I deserve to be mocked for being wrong. Now, I am sure the two of you have things to do, so I shall leave you at your peace."

Cupid cocked an eyebrow. "Is something wrong, Morph?" he asked.

"I just have a lot on my mind," Morpheus answered, meeting Cupid's gaze with his own impatient stare.

"Cupid and I are going to a new club out in the world," Artemis smiled. "Cleveland, was it? You are welcome to join us if you'd like. It might take your mind off things for a bit."

"That is precisely where I do not want my mind to be," Morpheus informed her.

"Wait." He considered her offer with a confused frown. "You are going to a club? You don't go to clubs!"

"Well, Cupid talked me into this one," Artemis answered. "I thought it might be a nice change of pace. Who knows? I may actually enjoy myself. I do enjoy dancing, after all."

"Not this type of dancing," Morpheus countered. "You are hunting something."

"Can a woman not simply go someplace without having an ulterior motive?" Artemis pleaded innocently.

Morpheus stared into her eyes silently for a moment longer. He then shrugged. "Perhaps," he said. "I still must decline your offer, though. I have things to do. Now, if you'll excuse me—"

Morpheus excused himself, without waiting for response. Artemis and Cupid watched him walk away.

"I wonder what he's up to," Artemis pondered.

"Who knows?" Cupid answered, turning his curiosity to Artemis. "He's Morpheus. I'm more interested in you right now. Was he right? Are you hunting something?"

"Yes," Artemis confirmed. "A good time."

Cupid raised his eyebrows, unconvinced. Morpheus was right: Artemis had never been one for the party scene. She had surprised Cupid by the invitation, but Cupid had accepted quickly, jumping at the chance to get out of Olympus, especially in the company of one of the original Olympians. As much as status no longer mattered as much, it was still an honor to be seen with one of the twelve thrones.

She was hunting something.

Artemis offered her arm, and Cupid took it. The two of them headed off. No matter what her motive might be, Cupid was looking forward to an evening with Artemis, relaxing and enjoying the club. It should be fun.

VII

The man with one sandal and the great bastard son
return to battle the false beasts of the new world.
Mistakes are made, and the Underworld returns one:
she will not be the same.
The three shall cause the power that was lost to be restored.

The Man with One Sandal was Jason of Iolkos.

The great bastard son was surely Hercules.

The term "false beasts" could refer to the automobiles the two of them had destroyed.

Lowering *The Posterus*, Morpheus' brow furrowed with deep thought. If Homer had forecast these events, what was going to happen? He seemed to be indicating the return of the old gods. No mortals remembered who they were any longer. There would be no point to them returning now, since no one would worship them!

Morpheus buried himself in the book once more. There must be something he was missing.

EPILOGUE

Passage through the Mists of Time is not as difficult as one might think. Really, if one simply focuses on their destination, it's easy to navigate. That is, of course, as long as the destination is straight ahead with no curves or detours. Once you throw in curves and detours, the journey becomes a bit more complex. Obstacles and distractions are inevitably going to be there.

The three sisters continued their work diligently, measuring, cutting, and cataloging the string. As much as they tried to ignore it, the newly restored string had caught all three of their attentions. They studied it very closely without even meaning to. None of them could understand why the string was restored. Still, it was not their job to wonder why. Their job was simply to pull, measure, and cut the string.

The Fates have always pulled, measured, and cut the strings.

The End

POST SCRIPT

A long, long time ago...

Aphrodite was dead. Everyone on the Mount had felt her die.

As Zeus walked the halls of Olympus, he thought over the latest, strongest attack their enemy had arranged against them. The slaughter of an Olympian seemed to have been their goal all along, and now that they had succeeded, there was nothing to stop them from doing more damage, both to the Olympian pantheon and to the world they had inhabited for so long. Their identities were still a secret, but it did not matter any longer. It made no difference who they were. The fact they existed, and they had so much power over the gods, was destructive enough. This was their world no longer.

Zeus entered the chamber, where the meeting he had ordered was being held. Everyone else was already there. Zeus scanned the room quickly, viewing the occupants. Within the room sat all of the Olympians, including Ares, still humiliated by his defeat at the hands of the Celts. Pythia, the Oracle of Delphi, was there as well. Her all-seeing eyes were now two empty, burnt-out sockets, herself a victim of an enemy attack. Apollo had assured her her eyes would repair themselves and she would see once more, but for now, her macabre gaze was more than a bit discouraging.

Seated next to the Oracle, as if replacing his mother, sat Cupid. He held the Oracle's hand encouragingly, as if there were any encouragement left to be had. He had been visiting The Oracle when the attack occurred but he had not recognized the attacker. Zeus suspected he blamed himself. Perhaps if he had been stronger, the Oracle would not have had her eyes burnt out. Of course, the more likely alternative was that he should have been killed or maimed as well. Their enemies had been suspiciously merciful.

Also joining them at the meeting was Hephaestus, welcome upon the Mount for this event. The weapon he had designed would never be used, at least not for the purpose it had been designed. It was a marvelous piece of technology, and Zeus was proud to say his son had built it. Still, even the most sensational development is wasted if circumstances negated its usefulness.

Zeus took his seat in the room, and all eyes were turned to him. He sighed deeply. This was not going to be an easy task.

"You all know why I have called this meeting," he began.

"We are going to war!" Ares championed his cause, rising ambitiously, still clad in his armor. "It is the only option we have; indeed, it has always been the only option! If you had seen it earlier, perhaps my sister would not be dead."

"Be quiet, Ares!" Athena roared, standing from her place in the circle and stepping into her brother's face. "You were the one who stepped out of line, violating the truce!"

"The truce should never have been made!" Ares screamed back at the only Olympian matching him in both size and strength. "It was a joke, thinking gods could happily co-exist. There will always be a battle for more power!"

"You were wrong, Ares," Artemis spoke up from her seat. "The symbols burned into Castor and Pollux' bodies were not Celtic. When you independently waged war against them, you ruined any hope of peace or cooperation that could have been found."

"It was never a hope," Ares snarled.

"Both of you need to sit down," came an uncharacteristically cold version of Cupid's voice.

Both Ares and Athena looked at him with surprise. Cupid's gaze never wavered. He met neither of their eyes as he lifted his coil of seasoned leaves to his lips and lit it. There seemed to be more emotion in Pythia's burnt-out eye sockets than in his chilling glare. Out of all of them, he had lost the most, and his demeanor reflected that. He did not look hurt and dismayed, or even angry... he simply looked cold. That, coming from the normally lackadaisical god of infatuation, was frightening enough. Ares looked as if he was about to snap back at the little upstart, but reconsidered. To the surprise of everyone, he simply returned to his seat. Athena needed even less convincing. Staring into Cupid's gaze, she felt a chill creep down her spine. Just as her brother, she sat back down.

"Thank you, Cupid," Zeus hesitantly said, nodding to him. If Cupid noticed, the only acknowledgement was an exhaled cloud of smoke.

"As I was saying," Zeus continued, "I have been thinking over the situation we find ourselves in. Perhaps thinking we and the foreign pantheons could all live in peace with each other was naive. That's obvious from the casualties our side has suffered. Ares may have been wrong to attack the Celtic tribes the way he did, without support and without just cause, but his premise was not completely faulty. We have been attacked, and the enemy remains a mystery, laughing at our pain.

"This is not our world any longer. Change has come, the world has moved on, and perhaps the time of the Olympians has gone."

"So, what then?" Ares gave vent to his signature rage. "We are simply supposed to kneel down and submit to our defeat? Do you expect us to simply bow our heads, being lead off like sheep to be sacrificed on the altar of this new world?"

"Hephaestus," Zeus did his best to ignore the war-god's critique, "can you explain the weapon you developed?"

"All right." Hephaestus nodded, trying not sound overly excited about his project. "I derived the idea from the river Styx and the way it sometimes will lead to the Underworld and sometimes lead to the other side. Dionysus' bar works the same way, where the people who know where the entrance is are able to transport themselves to the reality existing on the other side, but those who don't will pass the area, unknowing. As we all know, both the Underworld and Oblivion exist in a reality separate from our own, but still connected to an extent. Time moves differently there, and the events on Earth rarely, if ever, affect it. I began to explore other alternate realities holding the same parameters, and discovered there were plenty to choose from. Many of them had similar environmental structure and most were still unexplored territories."

Hera rolled her eyes. "Say that in Greek," she commanded. "I have no idea what language you are speaking."

"There are other worlds..." Hephaestus grumbled, turning a patronizing glare upon his mother, "and other people can live there.

"With this new discovery, I developed a portal system that would function as both a nexus to one of these newly discovered dimensions and a vacuum, creating a gravitational pull strong enough to entice the foreign entities. The idea was—"

"—the idea was to remove the enemy from the battlefield without ever having to shed blood." Apollo looked at Hephaestus with wide eyes and a dizzy grin. "Heph, that's brilliant."

"Well," Hephaestus turned to Apollo with a grateful smile, "the idea wasn't exactly to avoid bloodshed; it was to eliminate the enemy as completely and as effortlessly as possible. The lack of blood was just a happy bonus. I appreciate the recognition, though."

"A war without blood," Ares scoffed. "I have never heard a more ridiculous concept."

Zeus did his best to ignore Ares' comment. "This portal..." Zeus continued his probing. "The idea was successful?"

Hephaestus nodded. "It was," he confirmed. "In order to test it, I needed to send a living creature through the nexus and make sure they were still alive on the other side. With a little bit of manipulation, I was able to set up a system on one side to observe the events on the other. It was pretty complex, actually; I had to create a system of mirrors and reflective glass that would..."

Looking at the blank faces, Hephaestus realized he was losing his audience.

"I guess the details are irrelevant," he continued. "After I set up the reflecting glass, I sent a small dog through the portal. I watched, via the glass, as the dog emerged on the other side, complete and in one piece. The dog proceeded to run about the alien plain, through the grass and other elements, just as if it were still here. To be sure, I reversed the polarity of the nexus, and the dog was drawn back to the portal, coming out once more on this side. After examining the creature, I found it was in the exact state it had been before it had been sent through the portal."

"What does this have to do with anything?" Hera inquired, directing her question to her husband. "You have already told us we have no place in this world. What use could there possibly be for a weapon that—"

Hera's jaw fell silent and her eyes grew wide as she answered her own question.

"Could this portal be used as transport, instead of removal?" Zeus asked.

Every eye on the Mount, including the Oracle's burnt-out retina, turned to Zeus as the reality of what he was suggesting became clear. Zeus remained grimly intent on Hephaestus as his stoic head slowly nodded in confirmation.

The residents of Olympus were moving.

The time of the Olympians was over.

The world had moved on, leaving them behind.

Hephaestus had altered the machine a bit, making sure the alternate dimension they were going to transport themselves to was stable. He had also widened the wake of the portal to encompass larger and more concrete objects, thus allowing the Olympians to transport not only themselves, but their entire world. He had arranged for visual locations so they would be able to keep an eye on the world. Hephaestus agreed to keep the nexus open, so the gods could move to and from the world freely, providing they did not do anything to call attention to themselves. This was the only way Zeus would have allowed the exodus.

He needed to be able to reach the Earth.

Hercules had not returned. Throughout the entire ordeal, Zeus had expected his son to do so. He had been waiting for his champion to come and bring victory to the gods of Olympus. Perhaps Ares had been correct; perhaps they had been at war. If it were true, Hercules would have been invaluable to their ranks. They would have undoubtedly been successful, had he been leading the charge.

He was surely not dead. Zeus would have known it if one of his sons had died. That being the case, Zeus wondered where he was. For him to not have returned in their time of need, he must have been distracted by something important. Perhaps their enemy had abducted him, and he was being held captive right now. Perhaps he was being tortured for information, or perhaps their enemy had intended to use him for leverage over the Olympians. There was the chance he had been defending them all along, unknown to the Olympians, and that was why their casualties had been as slight as they had been. Maybe he had been drawn into a battle elsewhere, defending those who could not defend themselves. Hercules had always had a soft spot for the tortured and oppressed.

Perhaps he would return. Perhaps he would still be their champion.

Wherever Hercules was, Zeus knew he was doing something important.

Cupid
What's Love got to do With It?
(A Mythos Tale)
Introductory Disclaimer

I wrote this story as a Valentine's Day gift for the women who supported my webpage. On the "big day" (actually, about a week afterward, since it took a bit longer to write this than I had originally planned), I sent the story to each of them, along with a note from me, thanking them for their support, and wishing them each a Happy Valentine's Day. At the time, there were about 80 recipients, 70 of which I knew personally, and none of which I was involved with romantically.

The positive effect was that each of the women enjoyed the story, and most wrote back to thank me. The negative was that about half of the women thought that I had written the story, specifically for them. This lead to a series of awkward conversations, including one with an angry husband who didn't think the story was as cute as his wife had. In the future, should I do something like this again, the personal note will say something like "You're not special; I'm doing this for everyone," or I'll just make it a downloadable file on the website.

Since most of the gods in Mythos use their Greek names, a few people have asked me why I used Cupid, being Roman, as opposed to Eros. The short answer is because I thought featuring a well-dressed, cigar-smoking Cupid was cool, and if he had been called Eros, it wouldn't have had the same effect. The longer answer is explained in this story. Plus, Cupid's a lot of fun to work with, and I didn't feel like he was featured enough in the primary story. Developing his character was another reason. In the timeline, it occurs slightly before the main story. I hope you enjoy it.

—Jonny Capps

1

Early February is never a fun time in Northeast Ohio, where the sun seemingly takes a vacation. The temperature fluctuates between twenty-one degrees above zero and ten degrees below, sometimes within an hour. The impromptu holidays known as "snow days" thrill students, while simultaneously making adult workers long for the acne-filled, teen-angst days of high school once more. Road conditions severely deteriorate, but busy schedules refuse to accommodate increased travel time, leaving the owners of appointment books to adjust their timeline accordingly. Brief glimpses of a blue sky give residents hope that the hell of February will abate, but the idea is soon smashed by the downfall of snow, which occurs days, hours, or minutes later. February is not a good time for Northeast Ohio, nor for most of its residents.

Mercifully, February is the shortest of months, although it certainly does not feel like it. In the middle of February, there is a certain day individuals both look forward to and fear: Valentine's Day.

St. Valentine, the individual for which the day was named, had literally nothing to do with romantic love. He likely never had a partner of any sort, but instead was known for his charity. However, since charity is a difficult thing to market, the day has come to represent romance and passion. That being so, practically the only people who look forward to February are the owners (and their stock holders) of greeting card, candy, and specialty stores. Valentine's Day has come to be a day for loving couples to show how much they appreciate one another with cards, chocolates, stuffed bears, jewelry, and other tokens of affection, while the un-partnered are left to desperately look through their list of phone numbers, in search of another single individual who might spend the evening with them. Valentine's Day is a wonderful time for sturdy couples to affirm their dedication for each other, and for those who may be going through some trouble, to revive their passion. It is a sweet and romantic time, beautiful and loving. Since St. Valentine himself would likely not wish to take credit for this, most of the thanks can go instead to that cute, chubby cherub, with his whimsical quiver of heart-shaped arrows and his diaper.

2

The man stood in front of the card shop. The windows were flooded with images of the diapered baby and his bow, shooting hearts at the onlookers. In other sections of the windows, the effects of his arrows are felt through pierced paper hearts and other, similarly antiquated symbols of cliché-love. The man stared at the window in silence, his face downcast and somber.

"What the hell have they done to me?" he muttered to himself.

The man was not impressive to look at, but he certainly was not unattractive. He was nearly five and a half feet tall; short, yes, but not enough to be extraordinary. At first glance, his face appeared youthful, but a closer look into his frosted eyes betrayed a centuries-old pain. Dark brown strands of unkempt hair hung to his shoulders, which were hunched, giving the impression that he was shorter than he was. He wore a simple grey t-shirt under a pinstriped blazer, and a pair of jeans. A casual passer would never have noticed him, no, they would never have looked twice.

That had been the idea, of course. It was difficult for him to go unnoticed around Valentine's Day, particularly. When he had come to the mall, he had just wanted a few moments to himself to indulge in self-deprecation and resentment. It was difficult for him to blend in, particularly on this day, but up to this point, he had done it. However, while he was busy staring at the window in sullen frustration, he failed to notice he was not as unnoticed as he had thought.

"You've been looking at that store for a while now," a youthful female voice said from his side. "Are you trying to decide what you should buy for your Valentine?"

"Hmm," he huffed, trying to ignore the interruption. "No."

The young woman breathed deeply, as if embracing the atmosphere. "I just love Valentine's Day," she gushed. "Don't you?"

Finally, the man turned to view the speaker. It was a woman in her early twenties, if that. She was even shorter than he, but only by a fraction. Her unnaturally black hair hung to just below her ears, and chestnut eyes peered out from behind wire-rimmed glasses. She wore a black-and-white checkered blouse, above a too-short black skirt. Black tights covered her legs and, from mid-calf down, her feet were adorned in black, leather boots. Her deep-red lips smiled back at him as he smelled the aroma of manufactured allure wafting off of her. She was adorable, yes, but she seemed to be trying too hard to be even more so.

"It's a holiday celebrating the death of a third-century martyr with faux-romance and mass-marketing." The man shrugged. "What's not to love?"

"Oh, come on," the woman pouted. "Don't be so jaded. Do you have a special Valentine?"

The man returned his attention to the store window, sighing. "According to this store," he muttered, barely audible, "every Valentine belongs to me."

"What was that?"

"Never mind," the man replied, turning back to his conversation partner. "No, I don't have anyone special."

"Well, there's still a little time left." The woman smiled at him, endearingly. "Maybe you'll find someone!"

He saw the soft white of her cheeks suddenly complemented by a red tint. She was trying to seem aloof, but the twinkle in her eyes betrayed her. Maybe it really was time for him to have a Valentine. It could not hurt to give it a try, after all. It was surely better than being alone.

"I don't typically celebrate Valentine's Day," he replied, desperately fighting a smile that was creeping onto his lips. "Maybe it's time to break that habit."

The woman giggled as the smile finally broke through the man's defenses. "I'm Eve," she informed him, extending her hand.

The man accepted her hand, raised it to his lips, and kissed it softly. "It's a pleasure, Eve," he said. "You can call me... Erik."

He held her hand for a moment longer, watching the lights within her eyes dance. It was all she needed to enhance her beauty.

"You know," a new voice interrupted the moment with a flurry of rehearsed contempt, "it's a shame what this culture has done to the image of Cupid."

The man who called himself Erik turned to the newcomer with a quickly rekindled frustration. "Really?" he asked, coldly.

"Yes." The interloper, in a sweater vest with jeans two sizes too tight, nodded. "Look at that: a flying baby in a diaper? That was not how the god of erotic love was meant to be portrayed."

"You don't say."

"I do say." The young man ran his fingers through his disheveled hair and down the side of his beard. "Do you know what Cupid's name was originally?"

Erik regarded the interloper apathetically. "What was Cupid's original name?" he asked, patronizingly.

"His name was Eros," the man said, holding his head high, pretentiously looking to ensure that his audience appreciated his knowledge. "It was his Greek name, his true name."

Erik stared back at the boy, unimpressed.

"When Rome conquered Greece," the man continued, "they changed his name to Cupid, so as to avoid confusion between the two nations. However, many historians justify the reason for Cupid's bow as a tribute to his original title."

"Rome didn't conquer Greece, they—" Erik froze as the realization of what had just been said sunk in.

"Cupid carries a bow and... Eros?"

"I know, I know," the man chuckled. "It sounds lame now. What you have to remember is, at that time, puns were the height of comedic sophistication."

"Hmm." Erik nodded. "So, Cupid's a pun."

He began to walk away. It would have been pointless to correct the buffoonery, especially since the man had clearly only been looking for a way to begin conversation with Eve. Erik could think of nothing that he wanted more at that moment than to, once again, become unnoticed.

"Wait," Eve called after him. "I thought you were my Valentine!"

He continued walking, without turning.

"Well, that was certainly rude," the boy said, joining Eve at the window, and draping his arm across her shoulders. "It's a shame how inferior minds are intimidated by a superior intellect."

Eve glared at the boy in frustration, attempting to shrug away from his arm. "You just drove off my Valentine," she grumbled.

"Oh, you didn't need him, sweetie," the man chuckled, and tightened his hold on Eve's shoulders. "I'll be your Valentine. Don't you know smart is the new sexy?"

Eve looked at the boy, as he laughed casually. She was impressed by the fact that the longer she stared at the man, the less attracted she was to him. As he attempted to pull her closer, she shoved him away, aggressively. "Get off me, creep!"

3

His name was not Erik. That had simply been the first name which had popped into his head. It was close enough to his real name, anyway. Then again, it had been a very long time since he had used his original name. Maybe he should start doing that again.

After looking at the store window and hearing the trendy boy's idiotic rant, even thinking about the name "Cupid" made him want to wretch. Of course, considering it from a different light, the images in the window could have been considered flattery, in some demented, insulting way. Most of the other Roman gods had been relatively forgotten, their stories delegated to the same general category as "Snow White" and "Three Little Pigs," but considerably less popular. Cupid was still a household name. Few knew his stories or his history, but everyone knew who he was. Of course, everyone also knew him as a little cartoon baby with a toy bow, who shot cartoon hearts. It seemed a little over-the-top. When Rome had replaced Greece (since it was really a natural progression; "conquered" was too strong of word, especially considering the original Romans actually were Greek), they had simply adapted the Greek pantheon, probably out of laziness, to suit their own needs, and then designated new names for the gods. Thus, Ares became known as Mars, Zeus as Jupiter, and so on. Most of the Olympians had resisted the change, clinging to their Greek names (since Greece was cooler, anyway), but Eros had chosen to embrace the name Cupid.

Change was inevitable. Accepting it seemed like less work than resistance. Besides, he liked the sound; Cupid seemed like a more impressionable name. Judging from the store window, the assessment had not been incorrect.

He desperately wanted to smoke. With each step, the Brickhouse cigar inside of his blazer's breast pocket tempted him. Brickhouse was certainly not his favorite cigar. The lack of complexity sometimes made it boring and a bit tedious to finish. Still, it was a consistently nice and casual smoke. Right now, he was "jonesing" a bit. The interaction outside the card shop had damaged his calm. He would have pulled it out and lit up right there, but he did not want to chance it with so many people around him. Normally, he could smoke in public, unnoticed, but again, the card shop had caught him off-guard. It may have been a fluke.

Eve had been desperate for a Valentine. She had gone out of her way to notice a melancholy man, standing outside of a card shop, since that would have drawn her attention. The third party, overly secure in his pompous "knowledge" of mythology, had been noticing Eve, only seeing him through association. Reaching into his pocket, he fondled the cigar with longing. It was still better not to risk it.

A short distance away from where he wandered aimlessly through the mall, Erik noticed a tall, thin, well-dressed man, standing with a clipboard. Every now and then, an unlucky individual met his gaze. He then approached them, asking them to participate in whatever he was promoting. Most of the time, people shifted their gaze and ignored him as best they could. Occasionally, a person would stop, listen to him for a moment, then walk away again. Erik almost felt sorry for the man. He was working so hard, trying to talk to people, and he was clearly getting nowhere. It may have been because of pity, or perhaps because he needed something to distract him from the urge to smoke, but either way, Erik decided to investigate what the man was soliciting.

"Excuse me," he said, approaching the man.

The man nodded to him, stepping out of his way.

"Excuse me." Erik reasserted himself, stepping closer to the man.

The man looked at him curiously. "May I help you?" he stammered.

"I was just wondering what it was you're promoting."

"Oh, this?" The man looked at his clipboard. "It's just a survey we're taking in order to promote a new drug, which is said to help— did you want to take the survey?"

"I would," Erik nodded. "It sounds as though it could be fun."

"It is," the man encouraged him with raised eyebrows. "We're only promoting this drug today, and only at this location! You're in for a real experience!"

"Well, that does sound exciting." Erik laughed. "Lead the way."

The man motioned for Erik to follow him down a long hallway, toward an office door. Erik followed him happily. This was an excellent distraction!

NAME: Erik Smith

GENDER: Male

AGE: 32

ADDRESS: 222 B. Baker Street

NUMBER OF SUCCESSFUL ROMANTIC RELATIONSHIPS OVER THE PAST 5 YEARS: 0

WHEN ENTERING A RELATIONSHIP, DO YOU

EXPECT IT TO SUCCEED: I don't expect to enter a relationship, period. If one were to come along, it would be a shock, and I doubt very seriously if it would last beyond meeting my family.

WHAT DO YOU WANT MORE IN A RELATIONSHIP – MENTAL OR PHYSICAL COMPATIBILITY: There really is no good way to answer this question. If I say "mental," you'll assume my standards are too high, and that's the reason for my failing relationships. If I say "physical," you'll assume I'm shallow, and that will be your reasoning for the same result. If I say I'm waiting to find a combination of both, then you'll assume I'm a lost cause, living in a dreamworld (or that I meant to say physical, but didn't want to be considered shallow). Therefore, I'm just going to say "mentally physical." Yeah, try to define that!

AFTER A RELATIONSHIP ENDS, DO YOU EXPECT TO MAINTAIN FRIENDSHIP: Most of my relationships have ended when she died. Wait, that doesn't sound good. Where's the eraser on this stupid pen...

ARE FINANCES SHARED OR INDIVIDUAL: I couldn't really care less. I mean, I've got plenty of money, I don't really need hers. In fact, I should probably be collecting royalties from greeting card stores for using my image so frequently. Of course, that would mean I'd have to admit it's my image! I don't know if I really want to make such a confession. Plus, if I did get in a relationship, that'd mean I'd have to confess to her this is actually who I am. Let's keep finances individual for now.

HOW OFTEN SHOULD ROMANCE OCCUR IN ORDER TO KEEP A RELATIONSHIP STRONG: In the perfect relationship, romance should never end.

HAVE YOU EVER CHEATED/BEEN CHEATED ON IN A RELATIONSHIP: YES!!!!!

WHAT IS YOUR IDEA OF A PERFECT DATE: One where she doesn't even have to see me to know I'm there. She'll just feel my touch, and know she is safe with me. I can share myself with her, and she with me, and our eyes don't even have to meet. We'd be satisfied with one another, beyond the line of sight, merging our hearts and our minds on a level transcending visual stimulation.

HOW LONG SHOULD A RELATIONSHIP LAST BEFORE PROPOSAL: ...I'm sorry, I just saw my life flash before my eyes...

4

Walking from the testing room to the front desk, Erik handed his completed survey (five pages of relationship questions with very little rhyme or reason to the questions asked) to the disinterested receptionist. Without looking up at him, she accepted the results, motioning for him to have a seat in the waiting room with the other survey-takers to await his payment. There were three other men and two women, each with varying degrees of emotion on their faces. One man (6′2″, with dark hair, a broad chest, and muscular arms) looked anxious, as if the results of this test would tell him whether or not he should join a local chapter of monks. One woman (5′11″, blond hair, blue eyes, with a slightly heavy build) looked confident, as if nothing the test could tell her would affect her dating life in any shape or form, and she could still walk away with any man she chose. Erik sat in a vacant chair, smiled at the room's fellow occupants, and picked up a six-month-old magazine.

The articles did not interest him, but he needed something to distract him from the faces of the others in the room.

After waiting for roughly twenty minutes, and seeing the occupants of the room change to two women and one man, not including himself, his name was called. He chose to let the mystery of Will Smith's eternal youth remain unresearched, set down the magazine, and walked to the front desk, where the receptionist offered him a robotic smile. Sitting on the counter was a small, purple bottle, labeled *"Elixir leAmore,"* directly above the "SAMPLE" disclaimer. Erik did his best to restrain his curious cynicism as he approached the counter and returned the robot's apathetic smile.

"Thank you for taking the time to complete our survey," the receptionist said with all the sincerity of a two-month-late Christmas card. "Your participation is greatly appreciated. The results of your test indicate you could potentially benefit greatly from use of our new product."

Erik pointed to the bottle on the counter. "This stuff?"

"Yes," the receptionist confirmed. "After usage of this free sample, you should have sufficient information to make an accurate determination on whether—"

Erik picked up the bottle, studying it. "What's it supposed to do?" he asked.

"Our studies have shown that, through the use of this product," the receptionist continued without pause, "individuals have been able to establish stronger, more committed relationships, along with a more satisfying—"

"All of that, from this?" Erik opened the bottle, smelling the contents and inhaling deeply.

A fruity aroma wafted back at him. From the depths of the bottle, he could smell allure, as if it were a presence. It was a mixture of pheromones, stimulants, and other ingredients, designed to trick the mind into believing it was finding, or that it had found, love. The concentration of the ingredients was not strong enough to produce a lasting result. Even with prolonged exposure, the result would only be temporary, and it would only produce results on the recipient. There was nothing in the bottle that would make the taker any more desirable, aside from perhaps a placebo-version of confidence, and it certainly would not aid them in relationship development. There was one prominent ingredient, which Erik could not identify. It smelled somewhat like a chemical mix of lilacs and formaldehyde, shrouded behind a strange smell that Eric could not identify exactly. Looking at the list provided on the bottle, he was familiar with each one, suggesting that the ingredient was unlisted. This one facet remained a mystery. It hardly mattered, though; his analysis stood.

Closing the bottle, he set it back down on the counter. "This isn't going to work," he declared.

"Actually," the receptionist countered, "top scientists in the fields of biology and psychology have been involved in the development of this product. Their extensive research has shown that—"

"I don't care if the damn god of science himself boiled this up in his own private laboratory." Erik did his best to hold his emotions in check, while simultaneously remembering to breathe. "If I say it's not going to work, you can trust me on that!"

The receptionist's expression actually changed, proving she was not, in fact, an automated drone. Erik suppressed a smile at this discovery, knowing his humor wouldn't have been appreciated. The look on her face morphed into one of cold contempt.

"You do realize," she insisted, her voice holding all the warmth of a deep freezer, "that top biologists and psychologists, experts in human development and sexual therapy, have been heavily involved in the development of this product."

Erik nodded. "You have stated as much, yes."

"You're suggesting you are so much more qualified than any of those professionals that, with one whiff of the product, you can sufficiently devaluate all of their research. Who do you think you are?"

"I have more qualifications than they can ever hope for." Erik straightened himself, and thrust his shoulders back. "I am Eros."

As a rule, Olympians were not permitted to identify themselves to mortals. It made things too complicated. Eros had not meant to declare his identity so flippantly, but his pride at having his credentials called to question had gotten the better of him. Usually, he went by Cupid, but the image of the floating baby still left a sick taste in his mouth. Eros seemed like a stronger name right now. Judging from the receptionist's unimpressed stare, the name did not have the impact he had anticipated.

"What the hell is that supposed to mean?" she asked, dropping the last of her professional facade. "I'm Melody. Does that make me an expert, too?"

"No, you do not understand." The man formerly known as Erik scrambled to regain his footing. "I am Eros, the son of Aphrodite, the god of..."

As he spoke, the ridiculous notion that he was actually a Greek god from mythology, stories long since relegated to the category of folklore, sank into his head. She would never believe he was actually Eros (for more reasons than just Melody having no idea who Eros was). She would more likely assume he was insane. Eros quickly dropped the assertion.

"Forget it." He sighed. "It doesn't matter, anyway."

"Thank you for taking part in our test," Melody's robotic tone returned. "I'm sorry that our product was not of use to you. Good luck with your future relationships, and happy Valentine's Day. Have a good day, sir."

The argument was futile. Even if he had been able to convince her the drug was of no use in the construction of healthy relationships, she would have had no choice but to continue passing out the samples. That was what she was paid to do. As Eros walked from the testing room, his hand returned to the pocket of his blazer. The urge to smoke the cigar inside of his pocket returned with renewed force.

5

Ancient Greece had been the first culture to associate the heart with emotions. Other cultures had used the kidneys, the liver, or even the bowels. Eros tried to imagine how the music industry would have progressed without the emotional heart association. "Total Eclipse of the Bowels" did not seem to have the same poetic license. Terms like "you broke my kidneys" ... "my liver melts" ... or "put your bowels into it" also seemed less appropriate. The heart was a logical choice for the seat of emotions, especially considering the effect they had on the organ. Still, the heart is only a muscle. It serves as a pump, supplying blood to the body, and it does not have the ability to translate emotions. That occurs in the brain, specifically the amygdala. It was the brain that told the heart to beat faster, in response to stimulation, excitement, or attraction. The brain received the drug, oxytocin, which made people believe they were falling in love. Sadly, love had absolutely nothing to do with it, since it was simply the exchange of chemicals. In order for love, true love, to be real and lasting, it needed to move beyond the heightened heartbeat. It took effort, making the transition from short-term to long-term memory. In order for love to be worth it, one needed to work hard at it, committing to their partner, sacrificing themselves completely. Speeding up the heartbeat was a very small challenge. In a world that survived on 99-cent cheeseburgers, faster downloads, and text messages, it seemed logical this would be accepted as love.

6

After leaving the testing room, Eros hurried toward an exit. He tried not to take the insult very seriously. After all, the receptionist had no idea who he actually was. She probably would not have cared, even if she did. She was just doing her job, defending a product she was getting paid to promote. His insistence that he was not only an expert on the field, but more qualified in the field than anyone else, had fallen on deaf ears, as it logically should have. Still, he could not escape the feeling that this product belittled everything he stood for. The idea that this drug would lead to stronger, more stable relationships was a joke, especially considering it would not work.

He began to feel more and more like a junkie as he sped toward the door. His need to smoke was intensifying, and he needed a fix. Cigars were technically not physically addictive, but the maddening taunt of the stick in his pocket, which he could feel with each step he took, seemed to be calling the theory into question right now. He was a few yards from the door when he froze and turned. If his desire to smoke had been less intense, he likely would have noticed the anomaly sooner. If it had not been for the scent, he likely would have passed it completely. Frowning, he began to scan the area for the source. After a brief canvasing, he spotted it: a young African-American woman, clinging tightly to a heavyset, middle-aged man.

The two were obviously a couple. The desperate way they clung to each other, as if trying to broadcast the authenticity of their newly-developed feelings proved the newness of their relationship. The woman gazed passionately at the man, her eyes screaming that he could move mountains with only the power of his love for her. The man clasped to the woman tightly, gallantly protecting her from any dangers that would threaten her. They were clearly a new couple, but their passion appeared genuine.

Stranger couples had certainly been seen. No one would have even looked twice. Eros himself likely would not have bothered, had it not been for the smell. Wafting off of the two, like a cloud of invisible toxin, was the distinct odor of the drug.

Damn, Eros silently cursed. He really wanted to smoke! Still, he had priorities.

"Excuse me." Eros signaled for the couple's attention, approaching them quickly. The two of them greeted him with bright smiles.

"Oh, hi there," the woman returned his greeting casually.

"Yeah, hi." Eros nodded abruptly. "Quick question: did the two of you participate in that relationship survey which they're conducting right now?"

"We did," the woman confirmed, looking up at her partner with stars in her eyes.

"Thank God," the man sighed, gazing back at her.

"It saved our relationship," the woman swooned.

Eros frowned as he examined the couple. "So," he continued, "the two of you had a relationship before today, then?"

"We have always had a relationship," the man said, continuing to gaze at the woman in a dream-like haze.

"It was written in the stars," she replied, lights dancing in her eyes.

Eros frowned at the two of them with a mixture of confusion and disgust. "What is going on with these two?" he muttered to himself. "How long have the two of you actually been dating?" he asked the girl, trying not to make the question sound too much like an attack.

The woman sighed passionately, never looking away from her partner. "Time has no meaning while I'm with him. I could spend centuries wrapped in his arms."

Eros watched the couple for a moment. He felt bad for questioning the authenticity of their feelings. They seemed so infatuated with one another. It could be real! They certainly appeared to be passionate about the relationship. Still, there was something going on that did not sit right with him.

Testing a hunch, he turned to the man. "What's your name?" he asked, casually.

"My name's Yanick," the man said, never looking away from his partner.

"All right." Eros nodded. "What's hers?"

The man paused and, for a millisecond, Eros thought he saw sanity creeping in behind the cloud of infatuation. The next moment dashed those hopes, though, as the man answered.

"I do not need her name." The man sighed. "I only need her love."

"Awe." The woman giggled and blushed. "And I need only your hands, holding me tightly."

"I need only your image, held safely inside of my mind."

"I need only your lips, pressed against mine, giving me breath."

"I need only—"

"Okay, stop!" Eros cried in desperation before his ears started to bleed. A few other customers, including at least one similarly-smitten couple, stopped to watch the interaction. Eros quickly realized he was antagonizing himself, shattering their delusion, but he could take no more.

"This is not love," he continued his rant. "The two of you have never met before! You don't even know each other's names!"

"His name is Hero," the woman said, her full attention devoted to the man, "for he has rescued me from a life of sorrow and unrequited love."

"His name's Yanick." Eros threw his hands in the air with frustration. "He just said it!"

"Her name is Beauty," the man said, smiling at his partner, "for that is all which I see, gazing upon her."

"You two are absolutely disgusting!" Eros screamed, not caring about social tact any longer.

The girl turned to him and, for the first time since he had met them, Eros saw a different emotion: it was similar to that of a mother wolf, defending her cubs. "Do not hate us for what we have," she said, glaring daggers at him. "Simply because no one loves you, that is no reason to be jealous of those who have found true love."

Breathing deeply, Eros found his center once more. "I apologize for lashing out," he said, resisting the urge to step back, defensively, "but the two of you are not in love. What you are feeling is only a placebo capitalizing on your inner need for companionship, the environmental effects of the holiday, and the false confidence that the elixir creates. It is not true, it lacks foundation, and what you are feeling will not last beyond the effects of the drug-induced ambiance."

"Is that so?" the man sneered, as he squared his shoulders, posturing himself aggressively, as if preparing to hit Eros.

"Sadly, it is," Eros replied. If he was going to be hit, then there was nothing he could do to avoid it. He would not compromise what love was, and he would not stop defending its truth, simply to avoid an attack.

"If this feeling is false, then I renounce reality!" the man declared. "I have fallen for this woman's beauty, and the dreams within her eyes are ones I wish to share! I love this woman, deeply and passionately, and I declare now I always will!"

The man turned to the woman, and dropped to one knee.

"Oh, give me a break." Eros sighed, relieved that, for the moment, he had avoided physical confrontation.

"My dearest love," the man's proposal began, as he took the woman's hand. "I have spent my life searching for a woman like you, and the love she would show me. Now that I have found both, within your soul, I never want to be apart from you."

"Oh, I have waited for this moment, for what feels like forever." The woman gasped.

"Darling?"

"Yes, my love?"

"Will you marry me?"

"Yes! Yes! A thousand times, yes!"

The crowd of spectators applauded as the man stood, took the woman in his arms, and kissed her deeply.

"Do not encourage them!" Eros protested. The cheers, however, drowned out the sound of his voice.

"Do you love me enough to do something as romantic as that?" the female half of another love-drunk couple asked her partner.

Eros turned his attention to the second couple and, to his astonished horror, he watched the entire scene play out once more. The result was more cheering, more applause, and more madness from the approving mob. Scanning the onlookers, Eros did not see any other couples. He did notice, however, that the stench of the elixir was becoming overpowering. At least thirty percent of them, excluding the two newly-engaged couples, were under its effects. That could explain the unquestioning support that they showed for the impulsive decisions. Eros stepped back and watched as the two males approached one another and embraced in a brotherly way.

"Well," Yanick laughed. "I guess we need to find our fiancées' rings, huh?"

"Yeah," the other laughed. "I think Scotty's Galleria, the jeweler by the food court, is having a twenty-five percent off sale on engagement rings today!"

"Really?" Yanick's face beamed. "Wow, how perfect is that?"

"We couldn't have planned this better if we'd tried!" The other man was equally as excited.

"Come on, man, let's go!"

Taking the hands of their respective mates, the two men headed toward the jeweler. The spectators began to disperse, returning to their shopping.

"Excuse me." Eros stopped one of the non-drugged men. "Which jeweler is promoting the sale?"

Nothing about this was right, and Eros was beginning to figure out who was behind it all.

7

Bursting through the door of the testing room, Eros spun toward the receptionist's desk. There were two people still sitting in the waiting room, but that was not his problem. He waited until the man before him accepted the bottle of poison as payment for the survey and walked away, before approaching the counter. Melody was still behind it. Seeing him, she sneered callously.

"Well, if it isn't the Mighty Sniffer," she scoffed. "What is it now? Have you smelled the mercury our pens are leaking into the hands of our clients?"

"I need a—" Eros paused and frowned back at Melody. "How long have you been working on that line?"

Melody stared back at him coldly. "I don't need to script my insults," she sneered.

"Well, maybe you should," Eros replied. "Mercury doesn't have a scent. Look, I've reconsidered your proposed product and found my original assessment may have been too hasty. If the offer is still open, I think I'd like to try the sample."

"Oh, really?" Melody's face broke into a wide grin. "Have we met someone special?"

Eros blinked. "Met someone? Why would I need the—"

Remembering what the drug was supposed to do, Eros quickly cut himself off. "Oh!" he recovered as elegantly as he could. "Yes, I've met someone! She is far too beautiful, and our relationship is too important to leave anything to chance! I need your drug to make... to create love! It is important the love be real and authentic, and this drug is the only way to insure it is."

"Oh, that's sweet." Melody smiled a self-satisfied, patronizing smile. "Unfortunately, our free trial period just ended, and all of our free samples have been distributed already. You'll just have to use your charm and personality to win her heart, which shouldn't be difficult for you, being the expert you are. Just sniff her! After that, I'm sure you'll know exactly what to say to win her over!"

Eros chose not to mention he could see the people in the waiting room, holding the same survey that he had recently taken. He decided against saying he could smell the chemical afterglow of the drug on the boy he had been in line behind. He did not even bring up the box, full of unused samples, which he could plainly see behind the counter.

Instead, he reached into his back pocket and pulled out his wallet.

"How much do you want?" he asked, thumbing through a wad of bills.

"It's not a question of money." Melody shook her head. "The test is over."

"So, fifty bucks?"

"The testing period has completed, sir."

"Would you be willing to restart it for a hundred?"

Melody paused for a moment, and Eros saw consideration brewing in her eyes, but then she shook her head. "I'm sorry, sir," she said. "There's nothing I can do."

It was rare to find someone he could not buy off. This woman was intense! He must have really offended her with his former dismissal of the product. Still, he needed to get his hands on one of those bottles. Sliding his wallet back into his pocket, he decided on a different approach. It would damage his pride, but after the unfortunate incident outside of the card store, Eros did not imagine he had any pride left, anyway. Taking a deep breath, he closed his eyes to force himself into the mindset. Breathing out and opening his eyes once more, he leaned in and looked at the receptionist pleadingly.

"Please," he begged. "I'm sorry for the things I said about the formula earlier. I said them hastily and without thought. I have since seen the effect of the elixir in practice, and I've changed my mind. I have met someone, yes. She is beautiful, and I do not deserve her. However, I can't get her out of my mind, and she tells me she feels the same for me. She is too important to me, and I don't want this relationship left to chance. I need the formula to secure the authenticity of our feelings for each other."

Eros resisted a smug smile as his new technique had the desired effect.

Melody's cold and driven demeanor was beginning to soften. "This girl really means a lot to you, doesn't she?" she asked him, sympathetically.

Scanning his brain for an appropriate descriptive comment, Eros said the first thing that came to him: "She performs Swan Lake on the dance floor of my mind."

Eros' instant reaction was to gag on the excess mold on the cheese of that line. If he'd had more time, he certainly would have come up with something better! Swan Lake? He was the god of love! He should have at least come up with something a little better than that! He almost recanted his statement when a look into Melody's romanticized eyes told him not to bother.

"That's beautiful," Melody swooned. "I love Swan Lake! I wish my boyfriend could appreciate classical ballet like you do."

"I hope your boyfriend feels as passionately for you as I do for her," Eros continued, smiling dreamily, laying it on thicker and thicker. He was honestly surprised this young lady even knew what Swan Lake was! The receptionist looked at him, as if he were Prince Charming, battling fire-breathing dragons to rescue his true love from an ill-fated marriage. Her eyes never left his as she reached into the box behind the counter and took out two sample bottles. She smiled softly as she handed the toxin to him.

"The formula will work best if you both take the sample," she said, winking at him. "I'm sorry for my original judgment of you. I see now how real you are, and how passionately you care for this lucky woman. Good luck! I think you two will be happy together, I have a way of knowing these things."

Eros smiled as he accepted the bottles. "Happy Valentine's Day," he wished her, with thankful eyes and a slight blush.

Melody smiled as she watched him leave. She could hardly believe how wrong she had been about him! After all, it was natural to be skeptical of a new product. With this second meeting, she could better diagnose him. It was so romantic, the way he compared his crush to his private ballerina, dancing in his mind. What a sweetie! She was almost jealous of the object of his affection. She was a lucky woman. Men like him were rare.

Eros waited until he had turned the corner and was out of sight of the testing center to drop the second sample into the trash. He only needed the one for testing.

8

Eros walked quickly to the men's bathroom. None of the other men noticed either him or the drug in his blazer-pocket. No one makes eye contact in a men's bathroom. It was a sacred zone where men came, presented their offerings, purified themselves with "holy" water, and left. Social interaction was discouraged. That made Eros' job easier.

Stepping into an unoccupied stall, Eros closed and locked the door. Removing the sample-bottle from his blazer, he opened it carefully, as if handling hazardous material. The distinctive odor wafted up at him, nearly making him gag. Taking a deep breath, he brought the bottle to his lips, allowing a single drop to fall onto his tongue.

The taste reflected the odor: fruity, smooth, and chemical. Swishing the fluid about in his mouth, Eros began his analysis. As he had suspected, he immediately identified all the listed ingredients easily. The primary ones were on the top, the ones used to promote the illusion of love. They included the typical things used in many formulas to stimulate the oxytocin receptors and testosterone promoters to a simple degree. Predictably, there was much more of this than was needed. A lot of the drug's effect seemed to be due to the placebo effect, just as he had suspected. Underneath that was the artificial flavoring, which was pleasant and tasty. The company promoting the toxin had gone out of their way to make sure the recipients enjoyed the taste of their formula. There was nothing overtly manipulative or deceptive about the formula, at least not anything more than was usual, through the initial analysis. Spitting the contents of his mouth into the toilet, Eros carefully tasted another drop. Upon further analysis, he located the unidentified ingredient.

Through his interactions on Earth, he had become aware of energy drinks. Usually, he avoided the consumption, since he really did not require them. His body produced enough energy to keep him going, naturally. The drinks were primarily promoted to energy-addicts, mainly being teens and young adults, who thought that having more energy would make them more fun. College students were also heavy users, believing the drinks would endow them with superpowers, enabling them to remain awake through a lecture with a particularly monotone professor or stay awake longer to study for a midterm. The drinks were fairly effective, it seemed, and there was a large market for them.

Eros had succumbed to temptation once and purchased an energy drink. It had produced the promised burst of energy, of course, but the effect had lacked authenticity. It tricked the body into believing it had more energy than was actually present, and once the chemicals had worked their way through his body, it left a large deficit needing to be filled. Since the body had been working off of the pseudo-energy which the drink had provided, believing it had more energy than it actually did, the result was an even-more-tired feeling, with an immediate need for more energy. This goal was, of course, reached through an additional energy drink, made convenient by the fact one could purchase the drinks in packages of six or even twelve.

As Eros swirled the "love-nectar" about in his mouth, he quickly realized what was going on. Leaning over the toilet, Eros spit violently, making sure to get even the taste of the fluid out of his mouth. Dumping the rest of the formula into the bowl, he watched as the auto-flush feature swirled the toxin into the pipes below it. Racing from the stall to the sink, Eros rinsed out his mouth three or four times, just to make sure it was out. Leaving the men's room, he knew exactly where he needed to go.

This drug, mixed with the oxytocin/testosterone promoters, explained the effect he had been seeing. The formula was an energy drink, but instead of promoting pseudo-energy, it supplied pseudo-love.

9

BUY HER THE DREAM!
25% OFF ENGAGEMENT RINGS!
TODAY ONLY!!
STOP WAITING! THE TIME IS NOW!
No refunds or exchanges will be accepted for purchases made
through this sale

At any given time, there were three, maybe four customers in a jewelry store. Scotty's Galleria was not a department store, like Macy's or Sears, where people could find practically anything they desired. They appealed to a very specific clientèle: those seeking to purchase jewelry. Currently, the store was filled to capacity, with a line of people who were waiting outside. Eros considered the line. His theory seemed to be making more sense.

The sale was not out of place, considering the season. The fact that the sale directly coincided with the promotion of the "love-drug" could have been mere coincidence. Both things certainly seemed in spirit for the season. The fact that the store was so full right now could have just been a lucky accident for the store. Eros was not satisfied, though, especially considering what he now knew about the drug.

Eros studied the sales poster closely. The glowing ring and loud primary colors would certainly draw attention. A company posting the sale-stipulations in smaller print was certainly nothing new. It made sense from a business perspective: the sale would encourage impulse buying, and the company did not want to deal with possible remorse after any ill-thought decisions. The fact that very few of these couples would even remember their partner's name, let alone be in love with them after the drug wore off, was of very little concern to the company. Again, it could have been coincidence—or business strategy. Perhaps the owner of the company learned of the drug-promotions and scheduled his sale on the same day, on the chance something might work out. Judging from the line, if that were reality, it had been a stroke of genius.

"My baby wants this ring!" The aggravated voice of a male customer carried into the hall where Eros was standing. "What my baby wants, my baby gets!"

"Sir, I appreciate your situation," came the female voice of a stressed-out employee. "Unfortunately, we have just sold the last of that model. I can, of course, put one on backorder for you with a small deposit, or if you would prefer, I have been authorized to sell you this—"

"Unacceptable!" the man roared, followed by a wooden *thunk* as he slammed his fists down on the counter.

"—this model for an additional ten percent discount," the employee completed her offer with a heavy sigh.

"Ooo, I actually like that one better!" came the excited voice of another female, who was surely the male's temporary partner.

"I'll ring it up!" the employee said, brightly.

Eros frowned as he peered into the store. All three seemed overjoyed that the transaction was completed, although the employee was probably just glad to be rid of them. Eros considered approaching the couple to ask why they had compromised so quickly, but decided not to. They were very obviously under the "lovespell." The employee could have sold them a lump of coal on a gold-plated band, and they would have been satisfied just to have an engagement ring.

The "coincidence" theory was again called into question.

Eros shouldered his way into the store, in between rabid customers foaming at the mouth and telling him to get in line. He ignored them as he pushed through, artfully dodging the few who attempted to physically put him in his place. Through strategic maneuvering and ninja-like stealth, Eros eventually spotted an employee, the same one he had witnessed making the sale. Luckily for him, she seemed to have stepped away from the register, and she was currently leaning against a wall, about to hyperventilate. In her frazzled and worn-down state, she did not notice him until he reached out and touched her shoulder.

At his touch, she spun, like a velociraptor about to attack their prey. "Can I help you, sir?" she snapped. Her tone was so harsh that she may as well have said, "Back the hell off; I'm busy!"

Eros smiled at her genuinely. "Good afternoon, ma'am," he said, pleasantly. "How are you today?"

The employee, whose nametag read Lindsey, was unimpressed. "I am fine, sir," she answered with automated professionalism. "Is there something I can help you with?"

"I would like to speak with the manager, if you'd be so kind as to let him know."

"Sir, the manager is very busy right now." Lindsey rolled her glazed eyes. "If you would like to set an appointment, I'd be happy to—"

"I think I would rather speak with him right now," Eros asserted, the smile fading from his face. "I know what your company is doing."

"What would that be, sir?" Lindsey stared back at him, unblinking. "Selling jewelry at actually reasonable prices? Is that now a crime against consumerism?"

Eros stared deeply into Lindsey's stressed (yet intoxicatingly blue) eyes. "I know about the drug," he stated, coldly.

Lindsey's eyes quickly focused as all signs of stress drained from her face, replaced instead by surprise and slight horror. "One moment, sir," she said. "I'll let him know you wish to speak with him."

"Thank you," Eros said, smile returning. "I would appreciate that!"

Lindsey nodded rapidly before spinning away from him quickly. Eros watched with confidence as she retreated through a door behind the counter, which he assumed was the office. The response was almost instantaneous. She returned a few seconds later, motioning for him to come. Surfing skillfully through the dense crowd, Eros walked toward the door. He smiled his thanks to Lindsey as he passed through the entrance. Now, came the tricky part.

———

Eros walked into the room, taking a moment to take in the environment. Art deco hung on the walls of a lavish room. The floor was covered with a plush carpet, different from that of the storefront. A few over-sized easy chairs were scattered around. Quiet jazz music filled the air, along with the faint droning of the mini-fridge that sat in the corner. A desk sat directly in front of a large picture window. Behind the desk was an overweight man with a receding hairline. He smiled at Eros, in a wide, almost clown-like way.

"Good afternoon, sir," the man said in a jovial voice. "What seems to be the problem?"

"You didn't have the ring I was looking for," Eros said, casually, as he slid into a seat across from the desk.

"Oh, I'm sorry to hear that," the man said, dismissively. "As I'm sure you can see, we've had quite a bit of demand, particularly today.

Could you perhaps give me the specifications for the desired ring? I imagine we could find something similar."

"I'd like one I can return tomorrow," Eros replied, staring with contempt at the still smiling man. "You know, after the effects of the drug have worn off."

The smile dripped from the man's face like toothpaste slipping from a child's mouth. He looked back at Eros like a thief who had just tripped the house alarm. "I have no idea what you are talking about," he lied, unable to meet Eros' eyes.

"Really?" Eros smiled with a cocky flare. "I wonder if the FDA would know what I was talking about?"

That was a bluff. He had no intention of exposing himself to the FDA, especially regarding a drug-induced love-spell. That would be far too much of a risk and bring him too much publicity. He doubted, however, things would ever need to go that far.

The bluff seemed to have the desired effect. The man's head sank with a sigh.

"There's no need for that," he said, bringing his head up again and extending his hand. "My name's Bobby."

"I know who you are," Eros said coldly, ignoring the offered hand of "Robert Mammon."

Bobby jumped, startled.

"Your name is on the desk plaque." Eros rolled his eyes.

"Oh, yes," Bobby gathered himself. "Yes, I suppose it is. Good... good eye, Mr... I'm sorry, I did not catch your name."

"I have not given it yet." Eros sighed. "You can call me Eros."

His hesitation at identifying himself had been weakening, with each time people failed to recognize his name. It was true it only took one person to identify him, thus thrusting his entire guise into disarray, but he doubted that Robert Mammon would be that person.

"One name, huh?" Bobby chuckled. "Hey, if it works for Adele, why can't it work for you? I haven't heard Eros before, though. What does it mean?"

"It means you are not changing the subject," Eros replied, his glare intensifying. "I know what you're doing with this drug, turning people into love-drunk robots. This drug convinces people they have fallen deeply in love, instantly. What, did you suddenly have a surplus in wedding bands? What you are doing is perverse! Love should not be manipulated to serve your own—"

Eros paused to consider the irony of that statement, coming from himself. Daphne, Medea, even his own Psyche to an extent. How many times had he manipulated love for his own gain? This called his motivation into question. At first, he had been offended by the drug on moral grounds. Now he was beginning to wonder if he was more offended they were trying to play his game and, judging from the response, succeeding at it.

Eros reached casually into his jacket, gently rubbing the tip of his long-forgotten cigar. He wanted nothing more than to pull it out and start smoking it right now.

"There is literally no way to prove our company is in any way responsible for the distribution of that drug." Bobby sank back in his seat, attempting to regain his calm and control of the situation. "Your accusation is completely unfounded."

"Is that a fact?" Eros arched an eyebrow.

"Yes." Bobby nodded, finding his center. "And if you continue to promote fallacious slander about our company, we have the most powerful attorneys in America. They make a career out of squishing little bugs like you. You are completely powerless, and this meeting is over. Get out of my office."

Eros examined the angry man sitting across from him, pointing at the door. He saw an image of a little boy on a playground who nobody would play with, the chubby adolescent who took his cousin to prom. He was used to being pushed around and taken for granted. Here, in this environment, he was king, and Eros was an attacking army, threatening to take it all away. This did not excuse his behavior, or the product his company was promoting, but it did grant him a bit of sympathy. Eros knew that, in the pocket with the cigar, there was a small pouch, which contained his "weapon" ("Powder L'Amour," he begrudgingly christened it in his mind). With the smallest pinch of the powder, he could make this man do whatever he wanted. Something about Bobby, this red-faced, angry little man, made him reconsider. He would find another way to achieve his goals, or if not another way, another target. Without saying another word, Eros stood and turned to leave.

"Mr. Erress," Bobby called after him before he had gotten too far.

"It's Eros," Eros corrected him, swallowing his pride.

"These people," Bobby continued without acknowledging the correction, "are finding love. This is a love they wouldn't have felt otherwise, with the stimulant or without. Sure, it may be temporary—and I am not admitting any association with the product at all—but it's real for them right now! Why would you want to take it away from them?"

"Because love is real!" Eros spun to face him again, surprised at the passion in his own words. "It is strong, it is passionate, and when it's authentic, it's the most powerful force on Earth! When something is that real, no one should be tricked into accepting anything less!"

"Who are you to say this is less?" Bobby asked.

"I am Eros." He straightened himself and thrust his shoulders back, with as much authority as he could manage, while still feeling a bit like a hypocrite.

"And that means what to me?"

"Nothing." Eros deflated. "Nothing at all."

Without saying another word, Eros walked from the office.

10

When he first began his career as the distributor of euphoria alongside his mother, Aphrodite, Eros had used arrows as his medium, much like the degrading cherub who bore his name did. At the time, they had served his purposes well! It had been a time when magic was simply accepted, and the origins did not demand as much research. Originally, Eros had derived a formula from his mother's own concoctions, making sure to dilute it enough to make it more mild. He then coated the tips of his arrows with liquid euphoria.

Once his arrow struck the designated (or occasionally, the incidental) target, the formula dispersed throughout their entire body, filling them with undeniable infatuation for the individual within their line of sight. It was an inexact science, but it was the best he could do with what he had, at the time. As the world moved on and progressed, so also did Eros' available resources. As it became less appropriate to walk about with a bow and arrow, he had needed to develop a new, more effective technique.

After his mother's passing, Eros had needed to mature and to take his duties more seriously. While never officially appointed as his mother's successor, it seemed, at least to him, to be the natural progression. He modified his formula into a new, more adaptable product. With the help of Hermes, Eros converted the arrow-tips to a powder-like substance, which, when inhaled, produced an effect similar to that of the original.

The powder-conversion served his purposes well. He could now more easily gauge the potency level of the infatuation and, to some extent, the lasting effects. If he wanted a short, puppy love experience, a small dose of powder, used conservatively, would probably be appropriate.

A father wanted his daughter to fall deeply in love with a certain individual? Large dosage, spread over a longer period of time. The powder was also easier to conceal. Eros kept a small pouch filled with the powder with him at all times. It had been a good long while since he'd had use for it. Now, it seemed, he would be using it relatively soon.

11

Eros walked from the office, attempting to retain as much pride as he could. It was difficult, considering how he had been treated in Greece and Rome. He had never truly been a god people feared, but they at least respected him. There had been a significant number of people who had worshiped him. Modern American culture accepted Cupid as simply a diaper-wearing pudgy cherub with cartoon heart-shaped arrows. That was a step up from Eros, whom they did not remember at all. These were his two options: either be invisible, or be a fat baby, firing love-darts.

Perhaps it was time to take the name of Cupid back.

As he shouldered his way through the crowd of fevered consumers, who were spending more money than they had on things they would not want tomorrow, Eros noticed the employee he had spoken to earlier: Lindsey. She was still running ragged. She looked as though she were rapidly approaching a mental meltdown. Reaching into his pocket, Cupid produced the small pouch, held closed by a golden strand. Opening the pouch, he removed a small pinch of its contents. Smiling deviously, he snuck up behind her. It was time for Lindsey to have a well-earned break.

Eros waited patiently until she was done with the customer she was helping. Preparing the product in the palm of his hand, he tapped Lindsey on the shoulder. She spun on him, aggressively, like a pitbull, only much more attractive.

"Can I help you?" she asked frantically, with eyes practically begging him to put her out of her misery.

Quickly lifting his palm to be level with her face, Eros blew the contents at her. Lindsey coughed and stumbled backward, trying to blink the dust from her eyes.

"What," she stammered "What did you just do to... what was that?"

Eros smiled at her, demurely.

"Seriously." Lindsey glared at him. "Is that some kind of new perfume or something? Are you a sales rep? This is an incredibly busy day! How am I supposed to work if I'm stopping to sample your products?"

The smile on his face never weakened, as Eros locked eyes with her.

"I can't work like this," she breathed.

"Let me buy you a cup of coffee," Cupid said, offering his arm. "It's the least I can do."

"I suppose it is." Lindsey giggled, accepting his arm. "It's almost time for my break anyway."

The two of them delicately worked their way out of the store, walking hand-in-hand. As they exited, Eros heard the sound of the manager, yelling for her to return and for her to stay away from him. Lindsey did not even notice. Eros smiled.

He still had it.

The conversation between Eros and Lindsey was actually stimulating! Lindsey was able to maintain her composure. Eros had only given her a light dose; the effect wasn't extremely powerful, registering only as a slight crush. They both were able to enjoy a pleasant talk.

Eros had found himself not wanting the conversation to end, but there were things he needed to get done. Through the information Lindsey had provided, he had determined the drug was in an experimental stage, and this mall was the only one being used as a testing ground. If ever there was a time to destroy the drug, it was now.

The powder he had inflicted on Lindsey was in such a small dosage it was already beginning to wear off by the time they were halfway through their respective coffees. It was not an obvious letdown, but more of a gradual disillusionment. She stopped looking at him with stars in her eyes and began to see him with a more casual curiosity. By the time their cups were empty, the powder had run its course almost completely. Lindsey was prepared to return to her job, and Eros needed to proceed with his plan. They stood, shook hands, and thanked one another for an enjoyable break. Watching her walk away, Eros almost wished he could follow her. She truly looked as though she belonged on Olympus itself. Her raven-black hair fell like a sheet of fine silk, nearly to her waist, and the deep sea blue of her eyes captured the depths of a man's soul. As Eros watched her slender form walk away, he noticed less of a stride, and more of a glide, like soft, flowing water across the mall's floor. She was a different woman than the stressed-out employee he had met earlier, more liberated and free. Eros watched her for as long as he could, until she disappeared into the crowd, and continued staring in her direction, until he was satisfied she would not return. He did not do crushes, he repeated to himself, mentally. There were things that he needed to do.

12

As Eros returned to the testing room, where he would confront the distribution of the drug, he began to consider the conversation he had with Melody, the receptionist, only a short time ago. It had been manipulative and conniving. He had utilized the same tactics as the drug, getting her to emotionally connect with something that did not exist. This drug truly was doing the very thing he did. Perhaps that truly was what offended him most! This was his game. He knew how to play it best, and they should not be stepping on his territory.

Stepping into the testing room, Eros was greeted by the shining smile of Melody, overjoyed this time to see him once more. Standing next to the desk was Bobby Mammon, his face set in an unpleasant scowl. Eros locked eyes with him, and a chill ricocheted down his spinal cord. He was not used to such sensations! The venomous hatred pouring out of Bobby's eyes was almost otherworldly.

"Hi sweetie," Melody gushed, upon seeing Eros enter. "How are things going with your ballerina?"

"My what?" Eros stumbled over his thoughts momentarily. "Oh, right, Swan Lake. I don't know if we're going to—"

"That's the guy!" Bobby interrupted him, pointing his finger in Eros' direction. "That's the one who is trying to sabotage the formula!"

Melody brought her hand to her mouth as she gasped, her eyes expanding to twice their size. "No," she cried. "It can't be him! He's so sweet!"

"Oh, it's me, babe," Eros sneered, returning Bobby's furrowed brow with a cold glare. "Although, to be fair, all that I'm trying to do is uncover what this drug is actually doing. The drug itself is sabotage, isn't it? You are tricking people into believing they're falling in love, simply to make sales."

"You have no proof of that!" Bobby shouted back at him. "The only evidence you're presenting is circumstantial, trivial, not admissible in any court. Besides, you've yet to show any credentials! What qualifies you to know anything about the technique we're using in our drug?"

"What qualifies me?" Eros fought desperately to keep his temper in check. "You don't think I know the technique you've been using? You think I'm underqualified? I invented the technique!"

Bobby and Melody looked at each other in bewilderment. Eros took a deep breath, regretting the statement. He had practically just identified himself! *Oh look, everybody, I'm the great god of love, that's right, and you can't play my game without presenting the proper sacrifices, so you better stop it right now!* This was turning into a very unpleasant day. The unlit cigar was burning a hole in his pocket, almost making him cry.

"Were you one of the doctors involved in the development of the product?" Melody asked, logically.

"Yes," Eros lied, as he reached into his pocket to touch the cigar, reassuring himself it was still there. "Let's go with that."

His fingers grazed the golden strand holding his pouch closed. Inspiration suddenly hit him.

"You are no such thing!" Bobby growled. "You're just a bitter little man, trying to ruin true love for everyone else."

"It's not true love, you stupid son of a bitch!" Eros shouted as he pulled the pouch from his jacket-pocket. "It's not even a quality substitute!"

"You know nothing about love!" Bobby shouted back.

Eros froze. The rage in his eyes was enough to make Bobby take a step back.

"Hey man," he fumbled over his words. "I was just saying that you shouldn't—"

"I know nothing about love?"

"No, I didn't mean to—"

"I don't know the difference between true love and a false substitute?"

"That's not what I—"

"You don't think I know about faking love?"

"Maybe you should both just calm down," Melody said, nervously.

"You want to see fake love?" Eros emptied the pouch into the palm of his hand. "This is fake love!"

With a fluid motion, he tossed most of the powder into Bobby's face. Bobby coughed and blinked.

"What are you doing?" Melody gasped.

Turning to the receptionist, Eros repeated the technique on her, dumping the rest of the product into her own face.

"What the hell was that?" Bobby coughed, and dusted his face off.

"Is that some kind of new perfume?" Melody gasped.

Eros smiled at the two of them, demurely. In the back of his mind, he knew that he had just administered too large of a dose, but it was better to be safe than sorry.

"Look, I'm sorry about what I said," Bobby said, shaking his head to clear the cobwebs. "You're right, the company is using the drug to facilitate the sale of merchandise. They didn't tell me a whole lot, only that this one-day sale was specifically to coincide with the drug test!"

"Wow," Melody sighed. "Your ballerina is one lucky woman!"

"I knew something was fishy, especially when we started getting the line around the block," Bobby admitted. "I just didn't ask any questions; they don't pay me to be the morality police right?"

Eros continued to smile.

"I feel really bad about the things I said to you," Bobby confessed. "I mean, you were right all along. I'm so sorry. Let me buy you a beer to make up for it."

"Ooo, I want to come," Melody cheered, jumping up in her seat.

"A beer sounds nice," Eros admitted. "First, though, let's talk about what we're going to do about the drug."

13

A perfect ring of smoke drifted in the breeze.

Eros brought the cigar to his lips, taking another long draw. He had cheated. It was cheating, using his own drug to destroy the other. Timothy Leary used to say the best way to destroy a system was from the inside. It was similar to what he had done. By infatuating both Bobby and Melody so completely, he had created his own moles. The two of them had the power to bring down the entire system. It was cheating. He had done it to protect people (or at least that is how he would justify it), but it did not take away from the unfair aspect of what he had done.

Under the effects of his powder, Melody had agreed to flush the remaining samples down the toilet. Bobby had kept one sample-bottle, agreeing to never open it. He would accept returns from the drug-induced customers who complained and, should the company protest, he would contact the FDA, supplying them with the unopened bottle. Eros had, once again, cheated to achieve his goals, as it seemed he had been doing, ever since ancient Greece. This was a less selfish goal, or at least that is how it appeared on the surface, which served to alleviate his guilt. It had not really been cheating, though. Pheromones and infatuation were his gift, his "wheelhouse," of sorts. Could it really be considered cheating to use the skills he had been given?

Eros began to consider Bobby Mammon. When he had first noticed Bobby, he had been reluctant to use his dust on him, since it seemed like Bobby had grown up bullied and manipulated. Had Bobby not insulted him, he likely would not have dosed him.

Melody was a star-struck young lady, lost in her need for companionship and love. It seemed cruel for him to use the dust on her as well, making her believe she was having feelings she was not actually having. He'd had to dose her, due to her proximity to Bobby. She had seen what happened, and she needed to have similar feelings in order to go along with the plan. He was such an Olympian. Even after 2,000 years, it all came down to his hubris. He told himself he had done this to help people. How much of it was more for the sake of his injured pride?

Another puff of the cigar produced another fat ring of smoke. He was meeting Bobby and Melody for drinks in about an hour. Plenty of time to finish off his cigar and think about what he had done.

"So, cigars, huh?" a familiar voice met his ears. "How classy!"

Eros turned to see the young woman from earlier, Eve. She slid onto the bench beside him. He had been so lost in his thoughts he had not noticed her approaching.

"Well," Eros chuckled, relaxing a bit, "I'm a classy guy."

"Clearly." Eve pulled out a pack of cigarettes, beginning to search for a lighter. "Too classy for a common cigg-smoker?"

Reaching into his pocket, Eros pulled out his own torch. "As a rule, yes," he joked, offering to provide her light. "For you, though, I think I can make an exception."

Eve giggled as she lit her cigarette with his flame. "Such a gentleman." She blushed.

"Nah," Eros replied. "I'm a bad, bad dude."

"Most classy guys are." Eve smiled. "Anyway, our conversation was interrupted earlier. I was actually enjoying talking to you, before 'skinny-jeans' butted in."

"Skinny-jeans?" Eros frowned, and then remembered. "Oh, Cupid-guy! Yes, his pants truly were tight, weren't they?"

"I have no idea how he even was breathing!" Eve chuckled. "I think we should continue the conversation now. Your name's Erik, right?"

Eros shook his head. "Actually, it's not," he admitted. "My name's Er... you know what, my name is Cupid."

"Be serious!"

"I'm as serious as lung-cancer." Cupid laughed. "It's the name I was given, and it is the name I choose to embrace. So, babe, I guess the question you need to ask yourself is this: how would you like to be Cupid's Valentine?"

Eve laughed, choking on her smoke a little. Cupid laid his hand on her shoulder until she stopped. She was honestly interested in him, free of dust and of her own free will. It felt authentic, and it felt nice.

"That may be the cutest pick-up line I have ever heard." Eve giggled.

The two sat and smoked together, laughing, talking, and truly enjoying each other's company. As the conversation continued, the thoughts of cardboard hearts, flying babies, and manipulative drugs began to vanish. While Cupid knew he probably should not have used his true name, either Eros or Cupid, in such frequency and close-proximity, but right now, he did not care.

It was absolutely time to take the name of Cupid back.

The End

ACKNOWLEDGMENTS

A lot of people have been part of this project. First and foremost, my mother and father have always encouraged me to write and dream, so they're obvious. My childhood best friend, Joshua Margush, inspired me to create and never accept the world that existed in front of me as the only one. If I'm being honest, Josh is in all my stories: he's Jason, he's Morpheus, he's a lot of characters. My fellow author, DM Cain, introduced me to Next Chapter Publishing, and I'm very grateful for that. Cat Voleur has held my hand and sat beside me through a lot of dark times, and her belief in me has never faltered. It's also only fair that I acknowledge the YouTube content creators and Twitch streamers who have encouraged, entertained, inspired, comforted, informed, and (occasionally) annoyed me: Theradbrad, Markiplier, Alyska, bunnyrockets, Frickinjenn, That_Dahlia, agirlandhergames, and CelestialFitness.

See, I know there are more people that I should acknowledge. I'll remember, eventually...

Dear reader,

We hope you enjoyed reading *The Time After Oblivion*. Please take a moment to leave a review, even if it's a short one. Your opinion is important to us.

Discover more books by Jonny Capps at

https://www.nextchapter.pub/authors/jonny-capps

Want to know when one of our books is free or discounted? Join the newsletter at

http://eepurl.com/bqqB3H

Best regards,

Jonny Capps and the Next Chapter Team

Lightning Source UK Ltd.
Milton Keynes UK
UKHW040623141220
375159UK00002B/72